"Do you always loom over your prisoners like this?" Jasmine asked.

Wade was standing so close she could count the whiskers on his chin. He stepped back in surprise. "You're not my prisoner. I'm protecting you."

She stepped to the refrigerator and opened the door. "I don't think anyone camps out in freezing temperatures because they're protecting someone."

"I do," Wade said quietly.

"Yeah, well, Lonnie isn't coming here. He doesn't even know how to get here." She saw the doubt race across his face. "I know I could have told him how to find me, but I didn't. You're just going to have to trust me on that."

Jasmine wasn't looking at Wade, but she knew if she looked up she would see an expression of incredulity on his face. A lawman could never trust an ex-con, not entirely....

Books by Janet Tronstad

*Dry Creek
**The Sisterhood of the Dropped Stitches

JANET TRONSTAD

grew up on a small farm in Montana that had a barn, even if it wasn't big enough for an angel to swing from the rafters. Maybe that's why Dry Creek has a barn big enough so the angel can really fly. Janet has always loved a story that's better than life. Today, she lives in Pasadena, California, where she works as a full-time writer.

Silent Night
in Dry Creek
Janet Tronstad

Steeple
Hill®

Published by Steeple Hill Books™

STEEPLE HILL BOOKS

Steeple
Hill®

Recycling programs
for this product may
not exist in your area.

ISBN-13: 978-0-373-81431-2

SILENT NIGHT IN DRY CREEK

www.SteepleHill.com

Printed in U.S.A.

For unto you is born this day in the city of David
a Saviour, which is Christ the Lord.
—*Luke* 2:11

I have been blessed in my life to have some
warm, wonderful aunts (my mother's sisters).
This book is dedicated to them:
Wilma A (deceased now but I think of her often),
Grace L, Alice N, Mary M and Gladys B.

Chapter One

"You want me to keep an eye on *her?*" Wade Sutton pushed the café curtain aside and looked through the window to the only street in Dry Creek, Montana. Clumps of melting snow lined the rough asphalt road and the one vehicle in sight was an old motorcycle leaning against the corner of the hardware store. A tall, red-haired woman was walking toward that store right now, swinging her arms as if she was on some mission from God.

Wade grinned slightly as the edge of his hand pressed against the cold window. It was a cloudy December day and seeing the woman in her bulky, gray sweater and faded dress made his heart beat faster. He liked a strong woman and he could tell by the way she walked that she was a fine one.

Suddenly, a gust of wind blew the woman's skirt

up to her knees. She caught the material before it could go any higher. Now, that was the problem with all the piety in this small town, he thought. What was the point of a woman wearing a dress if she didn't show more leg than that?

Wade leaned forward to see if the wind would blow again.

"Nice looking, isn't she?" Sheriff Carl Wall said, moving the toothpick in his mouth. The two men were sitting in the café with their empty breakfast plates on the table in front of them. It was ten o'clock in the morning and the waitress was back in the kitchen. No one else was around.

"She's a regular movie star." Wade let the curtain fall into place and turned his attention to the other man. He knew the woman couldn't be as pious as she looked. Not if the sheriff had asked him to come up from Idaho Falls to watch her. "What's her thing? Stolen property? Blackmail? Arson?"

Wade was ready to sink his teeth into a surveillance job. Until six months ago, when he'd injured his leg while taking down some drug dealers, he'd been the busiest independent private investigator in the Rocky Mountain area. Now, no one except his old friend here was willing to defy the doctors and consider hiring him while he was still in physical therapy.

"Jasmine Hunter hasn't done anything," the sheriff said as he leaned back. "In fact, she even agreed to be the angel in the Christmas pageant this year, so she's real popular around here."

Wade remembered those pageants. "Then she's just plain nuts."

The annual pageant was held in an old barn on the edge of Dry Creek. The angel traditionally flew over the crowd with the help of a pulley in the hayloft. Wade had been the last kid allowed to swing as the angel. Now, it was always an adult.

"They've retired that leather pulley system you used. The pageant committee put in a whole new rope and wheel job. It's as safe as riding in an airplane."

Wade grunted. He'd take his chances with the old system; he didn't trust anything designed by a committee. Either way, it took nerve, though. Maybe that was why the sheriff had asked him here. "You want me to keep an eye on your angel so she doesn't skip town before the pageant? Is that it?"

"Very funny," the sheriff said without a smile as he leaned forward slightly and lowered his voice. "The truth is, I'm not worried about what she'll do, but what someone might do to her—if you get my meaning."

Wade didn't have a clue as to his meaning. The

sheriff's square, homely face didn't give much away. Wade hadn't been able to read Carl's face forty years ago when they were boys, so he didn't know why the man thought he could do it now.

"Has she requested protection?" Wade finally asked. The woman out there walking in the wind didn't look like she'd welcome someone stepping into her business. "I don't think anyone would attack an angel, especially not before Christmas."

"It's got nothing to do with the pageant. And no, she hasn't asked for help. She's too proud. That's why you need to be discreet, so she doesn't know you're keeping an eye on her."

Wade wondered what the angel was up to in her spare time. "This better be good. What is it? Abusive husband? Witness protection? What?"

Wade hoped it wasn't a domestic problem. The holidays brought out the worst in some families. He should know. As a boy, he never had a list for Santa Claus. All he wanted for Christmas was a safe hiding place so he wouldn't meet up with his grandfather's fists.

"There's no husband," the sheriff said as he leaned back again. "Not even a boyfriend hanging around. It's just a hunch I have."

The room was silent.

"That's it?" Wade finally asked to be sure he

wasn't missing something. It wasn't only a desire to get back to work that brought him here. His savings were almost gone so he really needed this job, but still—this was Carl. "I remember your hunches. They didn't always pan out."

"This one's different." The sheriff crossed his beefy arms. "You'll see."

Wade lifted an eyebrow. "Well, I hope you and your hunch are going to be around to post bail when this woman hauls me to court for following her around for no good reason. That's what will happen, you know. She'll call me a stalker. Just being worried is no excuse to put a tail on someone."

Wade didn't have much, but he prided himself on being a fierce defender of the law. He didn't take bribes, he didn't look the other way and he sure didn't violate anyone's rights by surveilling an innocent woman for no reason—especially not one who was as good-looking as that redhead. She wouldn't be the only one who would think he was a stalker; he'd half believe it himself. Even Scrooge would hesitate to put a tail on the Christmas angel.

"Now, don't go getting ahead of yourself. I'm not asking you to *follow* her exactly. She's staying out at her father's place—Elmer Maynard. You remember him? I just thought you could keep an eye on her. There's no law against seeing what's in front of your face."

"Elmer doesn't have a daughter." He remembered more than he cared to about his days growing up in this small town. The Maynards owned on the place next to his grandfather's farm so he knew them well. The man didn't have any sons, either.

"It turns out Elmer had an affair back when we were kids. Not that he knew anything about Jasmine until she showed up in Dry Creek last fall, fully grown and cruising past forty."

So she was around his age, Wade thought in satisfaction. Of course, that didn't mean anything. He made it a point never to socialize with church women and he'd guess she was a staunch one if she'd agreed to swing on that rope in the pageant. Besides, he was here on business.

He went back to the sheriff's comment. "I bet the tongues are still wagging over Elmer having a daughter."

Even as a boy, Wade knew how much Elmer and his wife wanted children. Of course, Elmer's wife was dead now so she would never know that her husband had a kid all along.

The sheriff shrugged. "People can only talk about things like that for so long. By the time

Jasmine found the three men who might have been her father and figured out Elmer was the one, well, people had sort of gotten used to her. And Edith Hargrove stood up for her, which helped a lot. She's Edith Nelson now that she married Charley, but I'm sure you remember her."

"Of course, I remember her."

Who could forget Edith? She was a warrior. When he was six, she had knocked on his grandfather's door and announced that Wade belonged in Sunday school. His grandfather had been too drunk to respond and Edith boldly took his silence for agreement. Every week after that, she stopped by to pick Wade up on her way to church. His grandfather never looked happy about it, but he didn't stop her.

Once Wade got over the miracle of someone going against his grandfather, he paid attention in church. For some strange reason, Edith saw potential in him when no one else did. Of course, he knew right from the start that he'd eventually disappoint her. No one could make themselves believe something they naturally didn't. Oh, he might have believed in God back then, but—like now—he just couldn't believe that God was of much use to anyone in this world. Frankly, Wade didn't trust Him.

The sheriff grinned. "Edith is some woman."

Wade nodded. "She's a force of nature, all right."

However, with the state of his bank account, he didn't have time to walk down memory lane.

"The problem is that you can't just pay me to follow someone around," Wade said, bringing the conversation back to what he needed to say. "Unless I'm in danger of getting shot, the county won't want to sign the check. They keep the safe stuff for their own people even if it means overtime."

Carl's face flushed. "About the money—the county doesn't exactly have a budget that—"

"Aww, man." Wade looked across the table at the closest thing he had to a friend. "You're joking, right? I drove all the way up here and you're telling me there's no money to pay for the job."

By now Carl's face was red, but he was sticking to his request. "Hold on. There's money. It's just coming from the city of Dry Creek instead of the county."

"When did Dry Creek become a city?" Wade glanced around in bewilderment. This café hadn't been here when he was a boy. Well, the building had been here, but it had been empty. There might be a couple of more houses behind the hardware store. And he heard they'd painted a mural on that old barn outside of town, hoping to get some tourists. He supposed it was progress, but— "It hasn't grown that much, has it?"

"We don't need to be big to have money."

"Enough to hire me?"

"Of course, you. We don't want a stranger poking around. And, if you're here, you can spend a few days at your grandfather's place. He's the only family you've got. Besides, he's having a hard time and it's Christmas. It'd be nice if you visited him."

Everything froze. Then Wade reached for his wallet. He'd pay for his breakfast and be out of here. "Christmas is just another date on the calendar as far as I'm concerned. If going to see my grandfather is part of the deal, then Dry Creek will have to find someone else."

"Now, don't be a fool," Carl said when he saw Wade's wallet. "I'm paying for breakfast. I know how it is when you can't work. And you're at least entitled to gas money for driving up here."

The sheriff pulled a wad of bills out of his jacket pocket.

Wade hadn't seen that kind of cash in months. "Don't tell me you carry that much money around. Is that the Dry Creek money?"

Carl flushed as he laid the well-worn bills on the table. "We don't have a checking account yet."

A suspicion started growing in Wade's mind. Those bills hadn't come fresh from a savings account, either. "Have you ever done this before? Collected money to hire someone?"

Carl was quiet.

"Well, that really settles it. I don't take charity," Wade said as he pushed back his chair. Pride was about all he had left and those bills told the story. Someone had passed the hat for him and he didn't like it. "You can tell everyone that I'm doing just fine."

The two men glared at each other for a minute.

"You can tell them yourself," the sheriff finally said. "If you're too stubborn to take honest work—"

"What's honest about it? I'm not going to follow some woman around just so you can give me money and make me think I earned it."

The sheriff's face softened. "It was either that or I'd have to deliver a carload of casseroles to your front step. You know the people around here help their own."

Just then the door to the café opened. Wade looked up and saw the red-haired woman walk into the room. A leather bag swung from her shoulder and the faint smell of some floral perfume swirled around her. As she took a few steps, he could see he'd underrated her looks. Her delicate porcelain skin was rosy from the cold and her auburn hair curled around her face, reminding him of a Botticelli angel with a halo. No wonder the people here wanted her in the Christmas pageant. She was like a picture in some museum.

And then she walked closer and he knew he was mistaken. She was too alive for a museum. Or any celestial gathering if it came to that. He'd never seen a woman like her. Her copper hair was spiked instead of curled like he'd thought at first. And her nose was slightly crooked. She wasn't the angel at the top of a Christmas tree; she was the angel who'd fallen just far enough off the top to be interesting to a flesh-and-blood man like him.

It was a good thing he was sitting down, because he felt a weakness in his knees. Suddenly, he wasn't so sure that he hadn't hit his head in the fight six months ago. He felt a little faint and his heart was acting up. But all he could do was gawk at her like the boy he used to be when he'd lived on the edge of this small town. That same feeling of watching his dreams from afar would pass, of course, but it annoyed him all the same. He didn't deal with dreams anymore in his life.

Chapter Two

Jasmine felt her breath catch. Who was that man? He stared back at her for a few seconds before looking down at his coffee cup. In the moment she met his eyes she could tell he had something to hide. At least that's what it must be because he went pale at the sight of her.

For a second, she wondered if he recognized her from prison. She'd told the people around here that she'd spent time in jail, but she didn't want someone from her past to come and remind them of it. Not when she was trying to be a normal woman instead of an ex-con.

She stood still as she looked at the man more closely. He had a fine-looking face, one she was sure she would remember if she'd seen it before. A dark growth of whiskers covered his chin and his moss-green eyes studied the pattern in the checkered tablecloth. His blue flannel shirt and jeans were both well-worn, too, as though he spent a lot of time outdoors. And he had a black Stetson hat sitting on the chair next to him.

If it wasn't for the way he held his coffee cup, she would think he was a new cowboy heading out to the Elkton Ranch. But he held his cup loosely. Her old boyfriend, Lonnie Denton, had held his cup that way when he wasn't sure what he'd need to do in the next minute or so. He said it gave him options. He could grab the cup and use it as a weapon or reach for the knife he kept in a sheath against his arm. He'd been proud when he explained that to her and she'd been sufficiently young and foolish to be impressed.

Jasmine mentally shook herself. She couldn't fall apart every time a suspicious-looking man came to town. She needed to leave her past behind if she expected others to forget it. And—most importantly—she needed to stop thinking about Lonnie. He was locked up tight in prison. He couldn't get out and, even though he'd always been unstable, she couldn't believe he would send someone to spy on her just because she'd sent him a pamphlet about heaven in the mail. Granted, it had been a colossal mistake; she'd known that when he had sent her that postcard in response. But that should be the end of it. She had a new life to live.

She looked at the man's sleeve in front of her. She couldn't see the outline of a knife sheath.

"I—ah—" Jasmine started to say and then stopped. She'd forgotten that her voice was raw. It sounded sultry rather than raspy, but her throat was sore all the same.

"Here. Let me get you some coffee," Carl said as he reached over to a nearby table and grabbed a clean cup. "It'll make your throat feel better."

Jasmine had been practicing her songs for the Christmas pageant a little too much lately. She'd taken a leap of faith a few weeks ago and pledged her life to God. She'd been half surprised lightning hadn't struck through the church roof on that day. In a burst of gratitude, she'd signed up to be the angel in the pageant.

She owed God big-time for taking her in. Doing the angel role wouldn't be enough to repay Him, but maybe it would be a start if she did it in some spectacular way. She was considering fireworks. Nothing too loud, of course, but maybe a sparkler trailing behind her as she swung over the audience would add pizzazz to the role.

She accepted the cup the sheriff filled from the

carafe and sat down in the chair he pulled out from the table he shared. Then she took two long sips of coffee.

When she'd been at the hardware store just now, she had picked up her mail. She was half afraid she'd get another postcard from Lonnie, but all she'd received was an invitation from the sheriff and his wife.

"Tell Barbara I'd love to come to dinner tonight," she said after she swallowed a gulp of coffee.

The people of Dry Creek had really taken Jasmine to their hearts when she volunteered to be in the pageant. Of course, she didn't have the courage to tell anyone that she'd never seen a Christmas pageant, let alone been in one before. Growing up, her mother had avoided churches and the only thing marking the season in their apartment had been a silver aluminum tree that was perpetually bent at the top.

The sheriff nodded at her proudly. "Dinner's going to be great. Barbara's got some fancy holiday menu going. She's been baking all day."

Jasmine swallowed. Things like that made her realize what she'd missed. Too much of her life had been lived behind bars when other women made Christmas dinners for their families. Not that she could afford to forget all that she'd learned. She opened her mouth to tell the sheriff about knives in sleeves.

"I'd like you to meet Wade Sutton," the sheriff said before she could speak. "He's a friend of mine—grew up around here. He'll be coming to dinner tonight, too—I hope."

The sheriff looked at the other man as he spoke and Wade gave him a slight nod.

Just then Jasmine placed the name. What a relief. "Why, you're the angel! I've heard about you."

The man slouched in his chair.

Jasmine hesitated. Maybe there were two Wade Suttons. This man didn't look like someone who would play an angel. He didn't even look like someone who would smile at the baby Jesus, let alone proclaim His holy birth from the rafters of the old barn. Of course, she'd heard the man was a private investigator, but that didn't mean he had to scowl all the time.

When she had heard the angel everyone talked about was coming to Dry Creek, she hadn't expected someone so solidly...well, male. Now that she was sitting, she could see the snug way his jeans fit along his thigh. Maybe he still had his leg in a cast that she couldn't see because of his jeans. No one had that much muscle, especially not someone willing to fly around on a rope. He shifted his leg slightly and she realized she was staring.

"Sorry," she muttered. "It's just I thought you'd look more like a ballet dancer. Because of the angel thing."

He shot her an incredulous look. "I was eleven."

She felt the heat of his indignant glare all the way down her spine.

"It's nothing. I was just wondering what kind of legs you had when you used those pulleys. Of course, your legs weren't so—so—" Jasmine felt herself blush. She hadn't blushed in years so she cleared her throat. "Well, the point is people are still talking about when you made your swing overhead. You had to be graceful. And your legs—well, I thought maybe you did something special with them as you made the swing. You know—the way you pointed your toes. That kind of thing. Really, I was just hoping you could give me some tips."

She didn't want to mention the sparkler idea. But even a clue as to the real part the angel played would be welcomed. Jasmine couldn't believe that all she was supposed to do was wave her wings over the shepherds and say a few words. Everything was too plain. She was coming to know a God who parted the seas and thundered from the rocks. He wouldn't have announced the birth of His Son without *some* drama.

"I didn't have much sense back then," Wade finally said reluctantly. "You should ask someone else for help."

"Oh." Jasmine said. He must have done something very special if he was so closemouthed about it. But, if he wouldn't tell her anything, how was she supposed to give a performance that surpassed, or at least equaled, his?

There was a moment's silence.

"How's everything at the hardware store?" the sheriff finally said a little too cheerfully. "I bet they're doing good business even in these hard times."

"I don't know." Jasmine didn't want to show her disappointment in Wade's response so she was glad the sheriff had started a new conversation. She turned to look at him. "There was a sale on nails. No one was buying, though."

"Things will pick up," the sheriff added. He seemed to be struggling with his words, although she couldn't imagine why. "People just need to be patient in these hard economic times."

Jasmine nodded. The pastor had asked for prayer for the store last Sunday. "I buy as much as I can there."

She tried to do everything that was mentioned in church, including the things that cost her money.

The sheriff turned a little more so she could see his face even though the other man couldn't. Then he winked at her. "There's no need to say anything to the people at the store about the hard times—they might be embarrassed."

"Oh, for goodness' sake, Carl," the other man spoke out. His eyes were smoldering and his jaw was clenched. "You don't need to warn people not to say anything to me. Everybody knows I'm the one who is supposed to get the handout. The people of Dry Creek just can't leave well enough alone."

Jasmine wondered how anyone had ever thought that man could be an angel. He might not even be suited to being the innkeeper, and that role was written for a surly actor.

"You should be grateful someone cares enough to help you." Jasmine refused to listen to any complaint about her friends in the church here. They were perfect—every one of them.

Although, she had to admit, they might have misjudged on this one. The man before her didn't look like someone who needed a handout. She had pictured him with the watery, timid eyes of someone who was ashamed of needing help. Instead, he almost bristled with pride. And, here she'd contributed six perfectly good dollars to the collection for him.

"I haven't taken a handout since I was a kid," the man said, and then pressed his lips together. "No reason to start again now."

"Well, I'm sure you can work enough to earn it if you want," Jasmine said. "There are still some parts left in the pageant. King Herod, for one. And you could coach me if you would just unbend a little and relax about it."

The man grunted. "Unbend? You should be worrying about things breaking instead of them bending. The church should get one of those mannequins to swing around up there for an angel."

Jasmine blinked. "A mannequin can't proclaim anything."

He shrugged. "Well, it's your funeral."

He wasn't suggesting it was dangerous, was he? She'd seen the pulley system; it was sturdy enough to swing an elephant across the barn.

The man's face didn't change, but he did lift his coffee cup for a drink.

Jasmine bit back her words. He was nothing like she'd expected. She wondered if God had sent him to her as some kind of a test. She secretly thought God should be a little choosier about who He let into His family, so she couldn't fault Him if He wanted to see what she would do when provoked.

"Wade here is Clarence Sutton's grandson," the sheriff finally said in the silence.

Jasmine summoned up a polite smile and looked at the man. "You must be staying out with your grandfather then."

"Not likely." The man's eyes flared for a second and then turned cold.

Apparently that scowl ran in the family along with his rather anti-social attitude. No one could accuse the elder Mr. Sutton of being neighborly, either. He lived next door to her father and the men had feuded for years. Still, Jasmine kept the smile on her face.

"He'll be spending the night at my place," the sheriff injected smoothly. "I expect he'd like to see some of the countryside while he's here, though. I figure he might as well drive out and pick you up for dinner. If that's all right?"

The sheriff smiled again.

"Oh, he doesn't need to do that." She wanted to talk to the man about the role of the angel, but she could do that in a few minutes. She didn't need any more time with him than was necessary, especially since he was so disagreeable. And arrogant. A man like him would probably think he was on a date with her if he drove her anywhere.

"You can't be riding that motorcycle at night," the sheriff continued. "I'd have to ticket you for not having your backlights working and Barbara would be upset with me. It could ruin the whole dinner. Besides, it might rain. Riding with Wade will at least keep you dry."

Everyone was quiet again.

"I might be able to borrow Edith's car," Jasmine finally said. Ever since Edith had gotten married for the second time, she didn't drive her old car very much. Sometimes the car wouldn't start right away, but Jasmine could get out and push it until it did if she had to.

"I can drive you," Wade said, and then added, "It'd be my pleasure."

He didn't sound like it would be his pleasure and that made Jasmine feel better. It definitely wouldn't be a date if neither one of them wanted it to be. And it was a cold night to be pushing a car. Maybe the test God was sending her was to see if she had the sense to stay out of the rain.

"I guess it'd be okay," she agreed.

At least the man didn't have bad breath or anything. And he nodded like he was a sensible person when he wasn't scowling. He might not want to tell her how he'd managed to give such a spectacular performance in the pageant, but if he sat next to her long enough, he might say something about it out of sheer boredom since she didn't plan to put any effort into making conversation with him.

The sheriff beamed at her. "I'm glad you stopped by. It reminds me that I need to invite Edith and Charley, too. Barbara wanted to have the two of you and another couple to balance out her table. Some notion she got watching Martha Stewart on television."

"Oh." Jasmine set her coffee cup down on the table. If the sheriff's wife was watching good old Martha, Jasmine needed to find a hostess gift before she went. She was sadly lacking in homemaking skills, but gift-giving was something important in prison, too, so she'd learned the value of that. "Well, I'll see you later, then."

Wade watched the woman flee from the café before he turned back to his friend. "Are you happy now? You've pretty much scared her away, making her think she's agreed to be a couple with me."

"Oh, she'd never think that. The women have her paired up with Conrad."

"Conrad?" Wade frowned.

"Nelson," the sheriff added. "Edith's his aunt now that she married Charley."

Wade remembered a kid by that name. He came to town during the summers to visit the Nelsons. Wade didn't think much of a man who relied on his aunt for matchmaking. "He doesn't seem like much of a go-getter in the romance department."

The sheriff snorted. "You should talk. I don't see a wedding ring on your finger."

Wade glared at his friend.

"Besides, I'm helping you set up your cover," the sheriff continued like he hadn't noticed Wade's look. "Lonely grandson comes home to be with his grandfather for the holidays. I can hear the Christmas bells ringing already."

"I don't need a cover." Wade gritted his teeth. "There's no reason to follow that woman around. I'm going home tomorrow."

Wade felt hollow the second he said the last. Who was he kidding? He never really thought of his apartment in Idaho Falls as home. His furniture was rented and all that the refrigerator ever held were takeout cartons and a few bottles of soft drinks and water. Half of the time he didn't even get his mail before someone made off with it, not that he had much to steal except pizza flyers and catalogs. All of which had been fine with him until he spent a few hours in Dry Creek again. Now he felt an old stirring, telling him there should be more to a man's life than what he had.

"I don't know," the sheriff said thoughtfully, and for the first time Wade saw real concern on his friend's face. "If she hadn't gotten that postcard last week, I wouldn't be worried."

Wade waited for more, but nothing came.

"Nobody dies from a postcard," he finally said.

The sheriff looked at Wade for a minute. "You remember Lonnie Denton? Shot a gas station attendant in Missoula twelve years ago?"

Wade nodded. "Almost killed the kid behind the counter. All for sixty-two dollars and change. I know a couple of the officers that finally picked him up."

"Well, Denton was Jasmine's boyfriend."

Wade whistled. He hadn't seen that coming.

"It was the only job she pulled with him and she called the ambulance that saved the kid's life," the sheriff continued. "She still got ten years prison time, though. Just got out a year or so ago."

That explained the walk, Wade thought. A woman had to be tough in prison.

"The postcard she got was from Denton."

Suddenly, the sheriff had all of Wade's attention. "I'm surprised they'd let him write to her— since they were in it together."

"He used a fake name for her. But he sent it to Dry Creek and she knew it was hers. She picked it up out of the general delivery mail on the hardware store counter. She showed it to me right away. Told me she didn't want me to think she was hiding anything. Said she'd sent him a pamphlet about the glories of heaven and this is what she got in return. I could see she was shaken, too. He said he'd see her soon."

Wade was quiet for a minute. He didn't like the thought of Jasmine worrying about the soul of a man like that. Not that he was overjoyed about the boyfriend angle, either. "I don't suppose Lonnie is up for parole or anything?"

The sheriff shook his head. "I found out where he was doing his time and called a guy I know who works at the prison, the one west of Phoenix. He said Lonnie had a seven-year stretch to go."

"I guess some people might say soon and mean seven years," Wade said.

"Maybe."

Wade had been an investigator for a long time. Partners in crime often stayed together. Something told him the woman was too perfect. She was trying too hard. And she was clearly nervous around him. All of that chatter about his part in that old pageant was probably just an attempt to distract him from her past. "How well do you know this Jasmine? Did you ever think maybe she and Lonnie are getting ready to pull another job and that's why he wrote to her? Maybe she's here to make plans."

"Jasmine served her time." The sheriff's tone was final.

"She wouldn't be the first one to be sent back to prison. Some folks find it hard to make it on the outside. Even getting a job can be a challenge." Wade stopped. "She does have a job, doesn't she?"

"She sure does. She works for Conrad in that mechanic shop of his. It's only part-time for now, but she's also keeping house for Elmer so she keeps busy."

"Isn't that convenient? Her working for her father and the man she's planning to marry—"

"Oh, she hasn't even gone out on a date with Conrad," the sheriff said. "And, whatever you do, don't tell the women I said they're thinking in that direction. My wife probably shouldn't have even told me. They don't want to scare her off."

Wade wondered what the women in this town thought it would take to scare a thief away from the full cashbox of a local business that was doing well enough to actually have employees. This Conrad fellow might not know it, but he was a target. Dry Creek wasn't Wade's town anymore, but he hated to see innocent folks being set up for robbery. He looked around. "I don't see a cash register here. I suppose the waitresses keep the money in the back?"

The sheriff narrowed his eyes. "I hope you're not accusing Jasmine of something."

Wade shrugged. "I'm being careful, that's all. Just because she's out of prison doesn't mean she didn't do what put her there in the first place."

The sheriff grunted and looked over his shoulder. "Just keep your suspicions to yourself. The women in this town will have my badge if they hear I let you get away with that kind of talk. Besides, Jasmine told me about the postcard. She wouldn't do that if she was planning something."

Wade picked his hat up from the seat beside him. "The real message Lonnie sent was probably in code so it wouldn't matter if you did read it. And she probably figured you would find out about the postcard and she told you so you wouldn't think anything of it. She was just playing it safe. That's all."

"But the people in Dry Creek *like* Jasmine."

Some people had probably liked Al Capone, too. "Of course, they like her. Nobody plans a robbery by going around making themselves unpopular with folks. It attracts too much attention. People watch unfriendly people. They write down the license plate number for their car. They remember where they've seen them. No, nice is a much better cover if you're up to something."

"I think you've been in this business too long. Nobody is planning anything."

"Does Elmer still have that fancy white Cadillac car of his?"

The sheriff narrowed his eyes. "That car is old as the hills by now. No self-respecting criminal would want to steal it."

"Well, let's hope not," Wade said as he pushed his chair back.

"She joined the church, too, you know," the sheriff added.

Wade nodded. That's just what someone would do if they wanted to gain people's trust, but he couldn't say that to Carl. His old friend had never been as cynical as he was. "I'll bet she's joined the choir, too."

The sheriff's jaw dropped. "How'd you know that?"

Wade just smiled as he stood up. He'd seen some sheet music in the bag the woman had on her shoulder, but he didn't mind looking mysterious to Carl. "Just doing my job."

The sheriff and Wade walked out of the restaurant together.

The cold wind hit Wade in the face and he pulled his hat down a little farther over his ears. The sheriff nodded and walked to the side of the café where he'd parked his car. Wade had to walk in the opposite direction.

It had been a long time since Wade had been in the town of Dry Creek. Back then the homes all looked like mansions compared to the weathered old house on his grandfather's farm. He'd spent his childhood feeling second-rate around the other kids here, especially at Christmas. His mother died when he was four and his father went to jail shortly after that, so the only one left to give Wade a present had been his grandfather.

Wade knew a gift was never coming, but it took him years to stop hoping. In the meantime, he was embarrassed to have anyone else know he spent his barren Christmases out in the barn while his grandfather drank himself into a stupor in the house. Maybe that's why he made up stories about imaginary Christmas dinners he claimed his grandfather used to make for them.

Wade smiled just remembering. Every Christmas, he had gone out to the barn and planned the stories he'd tell the other boys about those dinners.

He didn't want anyone to feel sorry for him so he climbed up to the hayloft where he kept his mother's jewelry box and her old magazines. That's where he found the picture of the coconut cake with raspberry filling that he said was his grandfather's specialty.

Wade had made it sound so mouth-watering the other kids practically drooled; he'd even agreed to copy the recipe for Carl one year.

But now, looking around at the houses, Wade wondered if some of those kids wouldn't have understood a hard Christmas. The town was very ordinary, maybe even poor. None of the houses were new and, even though each was set back from the main street with a fenced lawn, it was winter and no grass was growing. It felt strange to remember how he used to envy the kids who lived in these houses.

Fortunately, by now he knew a man could have a good life without a family. And Christmas passed just fine with a drive-thru hamburger and fries.

He shook his head slightly so the memory of the red-haired woman wouldn't sit so clearly in his mind. He didn't need to mess up his life by dreaming about her. She was like that coconut cake. Something nice to dream about, but nothing that was likely to ever come his way. He was glad the sheriff had tipped him to the fact that the women around here were planning for her to marry Conrad—that is, if the sheriff wasn't wrong and she didn't end up back in jail instead.

He stopped a minute; he didn't like thinking of her in a place like that. Then he sighed. His radar was good. That probably meant she was guilty as sin. Fortunately, it must also mean the church going was only a façade. If it was, he would have more in common with her than he thought. Suddenly, he was glad he was picking her up for dinner. It wouldn't hurt to get to know her a little bit better. Maybe she wasn't as much of an angel as she wanted people to think she was.

Chapter Three

Jasmine pulled the white curtain back from the kitchen window and looked out at her father's farm. She wished she could just forget about Wade Sutton. The view out this window usually soothed her. Late-day shadows made the deep red barn look almost black. Even though it was winter, there was very little snow. Behind the barn, a mixture of dried wheat stalks and tall weeds spread over the slight hill. Night would be here soon, but she could still see well enough.

Just looking out that far made her eyes feel restful after being in prison for so long. There were no concrete buildings or search lights in sight. Unfortunately, what her eyes kept coming back to was the new post on the hill. She could barely see it in the gathering dusk, but she knew it rose up in the area to the left of the barn where the barbed-wire fence trailed up the hill.

Most of the wire fence on Elmer's ranch sagged comfortably, but that particular section was stretched tight and kept in good repair. He said he wanted the divide clear between his land and the Sutton place.

Her father was a stubborn man. Clarence Sutton was another.

Several weeks ago, Clarence's old donkey had wandered out of its barn, down the road and into her father's lane. The animal had probably been looking for something to eat, but her father believed his neighbor had deliberately sent the donkey over to do mischief. Clarence, he said, always knew where his animals were and the donkey had a reputation for biting people. It had taken a bucket of oats to lure the donkey back to her barn and Clarence hadn't even come out of his house to say a proper thank-you.

Last week, in retaliation, her father had dug a hole and put a twelve-foot metal cross on the top of the hill that divided the two ranches. Then, as if that wasn't enough, today he'd taken several heavy-duty electrical cords and ran them from the barn up to the cross so he could wrap strands of Christmas tree lights around it. Now, in the evening, he could walk out to the barn and flip a switch and the cross would flash with white and yellow and clear lights. It would all look like a big golden cross that some televangelist would use.

Jasmine shook her head as she heard footsteps behind her. She turned to see her father walk into the kitchen from the living room. He was wearing jeans and a dark denim shirt with snap buttons. His white hair was plastered back and he had a look of glee on his weathered face. "Time to turn on those lights."

"Maybe you should wait and talk to Mr. Sutton before you do that," Jasmine said. "He might not like them and—"

She'd told her father she was going to dinner at the Walls', but she hadn't told him she was being picked up by Wade. The way her father fumed about that donkey of Clarence's, she doubted he'd be any more welcoming to the man's grandson. If everything stayed calm, though, there was a chance her father wouldn't see who was driving the car. He might just assume it was the sheriff behind the wheel.

"I'm celebrating Christmas. If old man Sutton doesn't like the lights, he can just look the other way." Her father picked a jacket off the coatrack by the door. "I got those special outdoor bulbs and I intend to use them—outside where they belong."

It suddenly struck Jasmine that the reason the people of Dry Creek might be so excited she was in the pageant was because they hoped she'd work a miracle between these two men. Maybe she should give it a try.

"It's not right," Jasmine declared when her father had his hand on the doorknob. "Christmas should bring people together. Decorations aren't something you use to annoy your neighbors."

Elmer turned to her. "Of course, Christmas brings people together. That's why I put the thing up there. Besides, an old sinner like Sutton should get down on his knees instead of complaining about Christmas anyway."

"You'll be using a lot of electricity with those lights." Jasmine tried a different argument. She didn't want to hear another list of Mr. Sutton's shortcomings. "And they're not energy-efficient bulbs."

"I've got nothing better to do with my money than pay the electric company," Elmer said as he opened the door. "I've already bought you that Christmas present and you won't take the rest."

Cold air came into the room.

"I'm practicing poverty," she said. She was working on all of the attributes of the Christian life. She'd found a pamphlet and she was targeting the hardest ones first. "I don't need more money."

Elmer had started to walk through the door, but he turned around to look at her. "That's why I'm buying you—"

"I don't need jewels, either," Jasmine added quickly. Her father had shown her the picture of a ten-thousand-dollar diamond-and-ruby necklace that he said he was buying for her. *Ten thousand dollars!* She hoped it was an empty promise.

"Every woman needs jewels," Elmer snapped back. "It gives her security. I should have given some to your mother. And my wife, too."

With that, he stomped out into the darkness.

Jasmine looked up at the clock on the wall. She didn't want to argue with her newly found father again tonight. She knew it was guilt that was driving him and she'd have a hard time making him understand.

She didn't care what holiday it was, real people didn't wear necklaces like that. Not unless they wanted thieves to buzz around every time they walked out of their houses. Besides, she wanted to walk by faith. Her father was wrong; a woman wasn't pushed to have as much faith when she had that many diamonds hanging around her neck.

She'd have to talk to her father later just to make sure he understood. In the meantime, Wade would be here in five minutes. She had planned to do a quick check on her lipstick so she stepped to the oval mirror hanging in the hallway.

She didn't know why she was making such a big deal of her appearance since this wasn't a date, but she wanted to look her best. Not that Wade would care if she wore a brown paper bag over her head. Her hand stopped. She wondered if she was guilty of the sin of vanity.

She sighed. She'd never thought there were so many pitfalls in the Christian life. Trying to make oneself worthy of God's acceptance was not easy. People kept saying God didn't care if she was an ex-con, but she just didn't see it that way.

Jasmine took her perfume bottle out of her purse before she realized. Of course, that was it. It was amazing that she hadn't seen it. No wonder Wade didn't offer any friendliness. She was an ex-con. He was a lawman. He probably saw them as oil and water; sin and righteousness—good and evil.

Well, that was probably best for both of them.

She went ahead and sprayed perfume on her wrists. She was determined to be like the other women in Dry Creek and she looked to Edith for inspiration. The older woman wore rose-scented perfume, so Jasmine kept with a light scent. Since Edith wore dresses, Jasmine had bought a couple of plain shifts at a thrift store in Billings. She no longer wore clothes with much color and she kept her shoes sensible.

Jasmine had started to go back to the kitchen when she saw headlights flash through the window. At least her father was still out in the barn. Hopefully, he'd stay out there until she was gone.

She pulled her coat off the back of a chair where she'd placed it earlier. Her coat was the one thing she hadn't been able to replace yet. Oh, well, she thought as she turned to the kitchen door, it would have to do. She shouldn't care what Wade thought about the way she dressed anyway.

Wade wondered what was wrong as he drove up to Elmer's house. On the drive out here, he'd thought nothing had changed in the decades that he'd been gone. The land was just as dry as it had always been and the gravel road had as many ruts. But he'd barely gotten out of Dry Creek before he saw a glowing light in the distance. When he turned off the main road to go down Elmer's lane, he saw that someone had put what looked like Christmas lights on a cross standing on the hill that divided Elmer's land from his grandfather's place.

Wade wondered why anyone would bother with lights way out here in the middle of nowhere since not that many people drove down this county road.

The one person who would see the cross most often would be Wade's grandfather. Those lights must shine right in front of the porch where his grandfather sat every evening about now.

Wade started to chuckle as he stopped his car in front of the house. So that was it. The cross would make his grandfather crazy. No doubt about it. The two old men had never gotten along. They must still be going at it.

The back door to the house opened and Wade saw Jasmine standing there. The day had grown darker and light streamed out the door behind her. Her red hair was spikier than it had been earlier and her black leather coat had what looked like metal rivets along the sleeves. She stood there a minute and Wade almost wished he could keep an eye on her like Carl wanted. Guilty or innocent, she was definitely his kind of woman. It would be a pleasure to watch her awhile.

He sat there, just enjoying the sight of her when—without any warning—a gunshot ripped through the silence. Wade looked over at Jasmine. She seemed frozen in place. With all of the light behind her, she made a perfect target.

"Get inside!" he yelled.

The sound of the shot had come from the north, so Wade bent down and drove his car as close as possible to the doorway where Jasmine had been standing.

"Lose the lights," he ordered when he saw they were still on in the kitchen. He didn't want someone shooting at the windows. He wondered if Lonnie had a problem with Jasmine and had sent someone to—

He shut off his car and opened his passenger door. Then he folded himself down and slid across the seat, stopping to pull his gun from the glove compartment as he passed.

Another shot rang out. That one sounded like it came from the direction of his grandfather's back porch and Wade relaxed a little. His grandfather was probably just shooting at a coyote or something. But a wise lawman didn't assume anything.

The night was dark and now that Wade's car lights and the ones in the house were off, he had to rely on his memory as he tried to sprint to the kitchen door. He hadn't run anywhere since he'd started therapy and his whole leg was throbbing in protest.

Wade twisted the knob and opened the door.

He stepped into the dark kitchen and something soft wrapped around his neck.

"A-a-rgh," he gurgled in protest. The only light in the room was an illuminated clock that hung on the wall and it didn't make anything but itself visible. The band around his neck loosened and he could tell it was an arm encased in leather.

He leaned back a little, preparing to make one of his defensive moves, when he realized he was settled into a womanly softness that was kind of nice. He was breathing better and, now that the lights were off, there was no reason to move. Besides, he could smell the perfume.

Maybe he got a little too comfortable in the dark leaning against her, because she whispered suspiciously. "Is that you?"

Now how did a man answer that? "Depends on who you're expecting."

He felt Jasmine shift her body as she took a step backward. Unfortunately, she didn't warn him and his body twisted to go with her. A muscle cramp in his leg seized him and he could hardly breathe. He clenched his teeth to keep from hissing in pain.

A small glow of light entered the room. Jasmine had reached back and opened the refrigerator door.

"Are you all right?" she asked now as she moved away from him slightly. "I didn't mean to hurt you. I was just—"

"Don't worry about it," he said hoarsely as he reached out to put his gun on the counter so he could massage his thigh. Now he could see why no one wanted to hire him until he'd conquered his leg spasms. He wasn't healing as fast as a younger man would. If a killer had been in the room, Wade would have been helpless to stop him.

"I'm sorry," Jasmine said as she moved closer.

The pain was leaving and in the light coming from the refrigerator he saw her misery. In the darkness, her eyes were pools of worry. He reached out and brushed her cheek, thinking to comfort her. "Who taught you about that defense hold anyway? You're pretty good at it."

"My old boyfriend, Lonnie," she whispered.

He could feel her breath on the back of his hand and it sent shivers down his spine. Then she looked up at him. She was beautiful. Without thinking, he bent his head down. She raised herself up on her tiptoes. He dipped farther down. He knew they were strangers and it was only the relief she was feeling that drew her close. But he was going to kiss her anyway. He just wanted to look at her a second or two longer before he did.

Then, without warning, the kitchen door opened with a crash.

Wade lunged toward his gun. He barely felt the pain in his leg, because of the panic inside. He'd grown soft. He'd assumed his grandfather had been behind the gunshots, but this wasn't the old man. He and Jasmine were going to die and it was all his fault.

"It's okay," Jasmine said quickly.

Wade thought she was talking to him until he saw the man in the doorway more clearly. Even with all of the shadows, Wade recognized Elmer as he stood there, looking ready to do battle, with a barnyard shovel in his hands.

"You all right?" Elmer asked as he flipped on the overhead light switch.

"We're fine," Jasmine answered as she stepped a little closer to Wade.

Elmer arched back like an attack cat.

"Who's he?" he demanded.

The older man didn't sound the least bit friendly, and Wade couldn't blame him. He carefully moved his hand away from the gun on the counter.

"He came to take me to dinner," Jasmine explained.

"He needs a gun to do that?"

"No, of course not." Jasmine took a step away from the counter as though she'd just realized a gun sat there.

"I'm sorry to disturb—" Wade began.

Then Elmer's fierce scowl disappeared. "Why

you're little Wade Sutton! I haven't seen you since—"

Elmer stopped and had the grace to look flustered.

Wade nodded. "Since the day my grandfather drove my dad and me away with enough shotgun blasts to rattle the entire county. As I recall, you were mending fence and had a first-row seat."

When he was fifteen, his father had come back from prison. He had lasted two weeks on the farm before he had a knock-down fight with Wade's grandfather. When his father left, Wade had gone with him. He'd never returned to the farm, not even to see if the new wheat he'd planted that spring had yielded the harvest he'd expected.

"Well," Elmer murmured. "You were a good kid even if you and your friends were messing with my Cadillac."

"You knew?"

Elmer grinned. "I could hardly blame you for wanting to sit inside. That Cadillac was something back then."

Wade relaxed. He was glad the man didn't ask about his father. But then everyone in Dry Creek must have heard his father ended his crime spree in a shoot-out with the police a few months after they'd left the farm. It was the day Wade had turned sixteen and he'd begged his father to take him along. He was so glad to have his father back, he would have gone anywhere with him. His father had refused, saying he wanted Wade to stay on the right side of the law and have a decent life.

"Your grandfather always did try to solve his problems with a shotgun," Elmer continued. "I figure that's him shooting at the cross. I saw one of the lights go out so he must have gotten off a good one."

If the shooter was aiming at the cross, it had to be his grandfather. At least that meant it wasn't someone like Lonnie Denton. "You'll have to report it to the sheriff."

"Can't be anyone but your grandfather," Elmer said as he studied Wade again. "The only set of lights coming down the road was yours. It's too dark out for someone to drive in unannounced."

Wade nodded. He supposed that was true, too.

"I'll give the sheriff a call after you're gone. No point in putting it off. I already unplugged the lights and your grandfather never leaves his porch until the seven-o'clock news comes on the television."

Wade remembered. Nothing gave the old man a better excuse to drink than the problems of the world.

"Yeah, well, I guess we should be going." Wade noticed that Elmer was still taking his measure.

Not everyone in Dry Creek would trust a Sutton these days, even if they were willing to take up a collection on his behalf.

"You take good care of my daughter," Elmer said.

Wade looked at Jasmine. Her face was flushed. He wished he'd kissed her even if her father had been crashing in the door. It probably would be his only chance and he'd always regret not tasting her lips.

"I can take care of myself," she said.

Elmer grunted.

"He's just giving me a ride," Jasmine continued. "I have some special lights on order for my motorcycle. I can't drive it at night until I get them."

Wade wondered why she didn't just say she was suffering his company because the sheriff had forced them to ride together. Carl was probably laughing his head off about it right now.

"You shouldn't be driving that bike at all," Elmer sputtered. "A lady should ride in a car. If you don't like driving my old Cadillac, I have a Bentley in the garage, too. And a few others."

"I do fine with my motorcycle," Jasmine said as she spread her hands. "I don't need *things*. Not in my new life."

Wade grunted. He wasn't about to ask any questions just now, but he did wonder what story she'd spun for Elmer. Everyone wanted things. He didn't trust someone who said otherwise.

"I've got my car outside," Wade said as he reached over to pick up his gun from the counter. He moved his leg again and grimaced in pain.

"Here," Elmer said as he held out a hand.

Wade took the help to steady himself. So this is what he'd come to, he thought. Depending on others like he was an old man.

"I forgot you'd damaged your leg," Elmer said. "That's why you can't work."

Wade tried to push the pain away. It was like he figured. Everyone knew about his problem. "I can get a job. Soon."

"Well, until you do—I put in twenty bucks."

Wade forced himself to give a short nod of thanks. He didn't want to have to explain to every person in Dry Creek why he couldn't take their charity. Maybe he'd ask the pastor to put a notice in the church bulletin offering to return the contributions. Maybe then they'd leave him alone.

"You need to take care of your leg," Jasmine said as she led the way to the outside door. She picked up a small jar of jam that was sitting on the counter.

"Hostess gift," she announced proudly.

Wade nodded. For someone who wasn't into things, she sure knew how to spread gifts around.

It was probably what made people think she was so sweet.

He picked up his gun and followed her to the door only to look back at Elmer. Apparently, Wade wasn't the only one feeling a little down. "Don't worry. She'll be fine."

The old man didn't say anything.

Wade opened the car door for Jasmine and she slid inside. They were at the gate leading to the main gravel road before he decided he had to know. "So was everyone there when they passed the hat for me?"

"Uh…"

"I'm a grown man. I can take care of myself." Wade looked straight ahead. The heater was going in his car and the dials on the dash were lit up. There was nothing but darkness outside the car.

"You should take the money anyway."

Wade looked over at her. He couldn't see her eyes in the darkness.

"You could consider it a Christmas present if you want," she added.

"If the people here wanted to give me a Christmas present, it would be socks." Wade suddenly remembered the many pairs of socks he'd gotten as a boy from the people in the church here. Sometimes, he'd also get a shirt or a jacket, too. Maybe that's why the money stung so much. He'd already received so much from these people. The kids might have believed his stories about the Christmas presents his grandfather gave him, but the adults knew better. They probably even knew there hadn't been any cake or turkey or apple stuffing.

"If they wanted to give me the money, they could have at least asked me to dig a ditch or something. That's honest work," Wade muttered half to himself. "I can't see where they think following the Christmas angel around could be anything at all."

"What?"

Wade heard the surprise in her voice and could have kicked himself. He was not himself tonight.

"They wanted you to follow *me?*" she asked.

"I could be mistaken," Wade said. "I—ah—it might have been one of the wise men."

Jasmine wasn't paying any attention to him. "I can't believe they'd ask you to follow me. What do they think—that I'm going to steal from somebody?"

"Oh, no," Wade said. Now he'd really done it. "The sheriff made it very clear that no one suspects you of anything. I was to protect you."

"From who? I can take care of myself."

Wade didn't know how to answer that. "The

sheriff had a hunch. That's all. He's worried about Lonnie."

"Lonnie's in jail."

"I know."

They were both silent for a moment.

"I don't need anyone to follow me around," Jasmine repeated. "I'm trying to start a new life and be a regular person—"

Wade had the alarming feeling she might cry.

"Well, don't worry," he said. It was the only comfort he could offer. "I'm not doing it."

"I should hope not," Jasmine said, and that was the last conversation they had until she pointed out the turnoff to the sheriff's house.

Wade knew he was leaving tomorrow, but he didn't want anyone to be upset when he did. Especially not Jasmine. He'd been stealing glances at her all the way down those lonely roads. He had the shadow of her profile clearly in his mind. He told himself it was in case he ever needed to pick her out of a lineup, but that wasn't it. He stole another glance at her. He just wanted to remember her.

"If you ever get down around Idaho Falls, be sure and give me a call," he found himself saying. "We could maybe have dinner or—"

She turned to look at him indignantly. "You don't have to ask me out. Or follow me. Or anything."

"Okay, well—" Wade knew when to step away from the firing line.

"Thanks anyway," Jasmine said, none too politely. "It was kind of you to offer."

It was crazy of him to offer, Wade figured. But he'd done it anyway. He supposed it was just because, back in the kitchen, he'd felt some emotion stirring. It was probably all that talk reminding him he'd once been the angel. He'd put that experience completely out of his mind. Who wanted to remember the time they'd mortified themselves in front of everyone they knew? But maybe some vestige of it had clung to his soul anyway.

He pulled the car to a halt in front of the Walls' house. The windows were decorated with Christmas lights and tall wooden candy canes lined the path up to the front door. Light and laughter spilled out the windows.

Even when he'd been in the pageant, he'd dreaded Christmas. Wade wondered if he was ever going to be on the right side of the holiday. He glanced over at Jasmine. He wondered if she knew she had a frown on her face as she marched up the sidewalk to the house. Then he realized he had one, too.

At times like this he wished he had someone to arrest.

Chapter Four

Jasmine had lost what little Christmas cheer she had. She was sitting on the sofa in the Walls' living room with a glass of cold spiced cider in one hand and a piece of stuffed celery in the other. Carols were playing on the stereo system and she'd just let her misery overflow to Edith, the only other person in the room. The older woman was sitting next to her on a straight-backed oak chair.

"Oh, dear, no, we'd never pay someone to take you out," Edith protested.

"Not take me out," Jasmine corrected in the whisper she'd been using to tell the story. "Follow me around."

"Oh, Wade wouldn't do that. Goodness, no. You must have heard him wrong." Edith's short gray hair was tightly permed and her waves shook along with her head. She had a worried look on her kindly face and her white magnetic necklace hung above a red checked housedress in an attempt at seasonal fashion. "Besides, Wade isn't the man we have in mind for you anyway."

"You have someone in mind for me?" Jasmine looked around to be sure no one else had walked back into the living room. It sounded like they were all still in the kitchen putting the finishing touches on that coconut cake.

"Well, just Conrad. You know he's a sweet man. A little shy maybe, but… Of course, it's just a suggestion. For when you're ready to date."

"I don't need to date anyone," Jasmine said firmly. She supposed a husband like Conrad made sense given the fact that she wanted a regular life. But somehow the prospect seemed a little suffocating right now. Of course, he was a good mechanic. She liked that, but— "No one needs to worry about me. Maybe Wade can do whatever he's supposed to do with someone else."

"Yes, well, maybe. I thought he was going to help the sheriff, though," Edith conceded as she rubbed her hand around her wrist. "Maybe he could be a security guard at the barn now that we're setting up the stage. With the pageant being this Monday—"

"Do you want an aspirin?" Jasmine asked. Everyone knew the older woman suffered from arthritis on cold evenings. Her wrist must be hurting.

Edith shook her head. "I'll be fine. And don't worry about Wade. I'm sure it's just a misunderstanding."

"He said he'd rather dig ditches than have anything to do with me." Jasmine didn't realize how peevish she sounded until she saw a spark of interest light up her friend's eyes.

"Not that I want him to," Jasmine added firmly. "He's just a test from God anyway."

Edith looked a little startled. "In what way?"

Jasmine wished she'd left that last part out. "Oh, you know, old feelings."

She'd already decided that, when she'd almost kissed him in her father's kitchen, it had just been because of the rush of adrenaline that had raced through her after the gunshots. It was a natural response. Guns always made her nervous these days. It had nothing to do with the way Wade's eyes made her feel. Or the way the line of his chin looked so strong. Or—

"I don't know that God sends us people as tests," Edith said gently, interrupting her thoughts.

They were silent for a moment, Jasmine taking a sip of her cider and Edith taking a drink from the glass of water by her side.

"I must admit Wade's a handsome man," Edith finally said. "I can see why you'd be interested."

"I'm not—"

Edith just kept going. "The problem is that he has it in his head he can't really trust anyone. He refuses to even have a partner on the job. Until he does, I can't see him being married. Not happily. And he doesn't have much use for God, either. I blame myself for that."

"You?" Jasmine set her glass of cider down. "How can it possibly be your fault?"

"I should have taken him to live with me and my husband. It wasn't good for him to rattle around in that house with his grandfather. The man wasn't even sober most of the time. He would have given the boy up for a case of cheap wine. I thought a couple of times of making him an offer, but I kept hoping things would get better. How could a boy, living with someone like that, trust anyone?"

"He looks like he turned out fine." Jasmine offered what comfort she could.

"Yes, in some ways," Edith said slowly. "Carl says he's got a spotless reputation. Determined and smart. He never bends the rules. Always by the book. Other lawmen look up to him."

Jasmine swallowed. She wondered why a man like that had been tempted to kiss her.

"He's a good boy," Edith finished. "Even if he hasn't answered the letter I wrote him about his grandfather."

"It sounds like Mr. Sutton cooked some grand meals in his time." Jasmine grabbed at a new topic like a lifeline. She'd been in the kitchen earlier when Barbara had been asking Wade about the cake his grandfather used to bake. The raspberry filling apparently had orange flavoring in it, too.

"That cake is the very reason I should have taken Wade in. I knew back then it was too good to be true."

Just then a burst of laughter came from the kitchen.

"Sounds like they're having fun," Jasmine said.

Edith nodded and started to stand up. "No point in us sitting out here when the excitement's in there."

Wade was holding the frosting spoon in his hand, feeling like a fraud. Carl's two kids had taken Charley outside to see their kittens and he and Carl were standing at the center counter in the kitchen. Two round circles of white cake sat on wire racks. A bowl of raspberries sat beside them.

Carl's petite, dark-haired wife, Barbara, said she'd followed Carl's crumpled up old recipe as best she could but that she had waited for Wade to get there to assemble the Christmas Fantasy Cake. He'd been dumbstruck that she'd baked it.

"You say your grandfather found the cake in a magazine?" Barbara was asking as she turned the bowl of icing slightly. She was standing at the side counter so she'd have room to move around the cake. "I hope that you don't mind that I named it. Did your grandfather call it anything special?"

"All I know is there was a picture of it in *Good Housekeeping.*" Wade remembered his mother's magazine like he'd been holding it yesterday. It was the one thing in the whole story that was true. He wondered how he was going to carefully unravel his lies without destroying Barbara's enthusiasm. "My grandfather really wasn't much of a cook."

"Well, maybe not every day, but on Christmas. Uhmmm," Carl said with a smile as he looked down at his Barbara with love in his eyes. "I used to spend half of Christmas thinking about Wade over there eating that cake. I wished my mother's fruitcake was half as good. And then I found you and you made the cake for us."

Carl gave his wife a quick kiss. "You're a great cook."

Wade felt hollow. "I may have exaggerated the cake back then."

"I wondered how you got the fresh raspberries

for the filling," Barbara said with a smile. Her face was pink with pleasure from the kiss she'd received. "Carl insisted they had to be fresh, but all I could find was frozen."

Just then Edith and Jasmine walked into the kitchen.

Barbara turned to Edith. "Do raspberries grow wild around here at all? I know the chokecherries do and I've heard of some wild strawberries over by the Redfern place."

Wade knew he was in trouble. Edith had been inside his grandfather's house. The top of the stove had always been piled high with empty liquor bottles. She must know the stories of cake and turkey dinners had been false. His grandfather could barely make toast. Wade had lived on peanut butter sandwiches and the bruised apples his grandfather bought by the case from a wholesale place in Washington.

"I think raspberries always have to be tended," Edith said.

Wade didn't like standing there knowing she knew he was a fake. But, on the other hand, Barbara was looking proud and content in her ruffled white apron. The smell of the freshly baked cake was still in the air and the frosting was on the spoon she'd given him to taste.

Carl shook the jar of coconut. "Yeah, I always wondered about the fresh raspberries, too. How did your grandfather manage to get them?"

"This whole thing, well—it's—" Wade looked around. He couldn't find words to say what he needed to say so he compromised. "I hope you know how touched I am by this even though it's not really necessary. The truth is—"

Carl stopped him with a hand on his shoulder. "No need to thank us. Just thinking about your grandfather making this cake tells me he has a soft side. That's the first thing I thought of when Elmer called to say your grandfather was shooting at that cross. I said to myself that Clarence Sutton is a good man, deep down inside. I don't think we need to put him in jail—especially not with Christmas only a few days away."

"You don't?" Wade asked in surprise. "Because he'll do it again."

Carl shook his head. "Not if we arrange for him to be under house arrest. And we'll take away his gun. He should have someone checking in on him anyway."

"I don't—" Wade felt the weight of everything. Did he have an obligation? The man had chased him away with his shotgun over twenty-five years ago.

"Oh, not you," Carl said quickly. "We'll have to find someone. That's all."

Everyone was silent. Barbara went back to putting the raspberry filling on top of one of the white cake layers. Wade was trying to think of words to steer the conversation back to the confession he needed to make. It didn't help that Jasmine was there, staring at him like he'd done something wrong.

He was trying not to look at her, but he could see her out of the corner of his eye and he had to stop his head from moving in her direction. He wondered if she thought he had been taking advantage of the situation when he tried to kiss her. Of course, he had been—he'd been doomed to foolishness when he first looked in her eyes.

"Maybe the Covered Dish Ladies could check on Mr. Sutton," Edith finally said. "I mean, we need to go over there anyway—and we understand his problems."

Wade brought himself back to the present. What was she saying? As far as he knew, his grandfather didn't have any problems that required something as sensitive as understanding. Sympathy didn't do much for a drunk. Edith should know that.

"I can hardly deputize you," the sheriff said. "You're all ladies."

"We're not all ladies," Jasmine offered. "I could take a turn delivering something. He's just an old man. Besides, I'd know what to do if—if he started shooting."

"No," Wade said at the same time as the sheriff did.

"If I can't do it," the sheriff said as he handed the jar of coconut to his wife. "I'll ask one of the deputies to come down from Miles City tomorrow."

Wade felt low. He barely remembered the Covered Dish Ladies. They were some kind of woman's group at the church. He couldn't recall what they did, but he supposed they got together and made Christmas cookies or something for the baskets they handed out over the holidays. His grandfather must be on their list for sugar cookies. And, now the old man was on the deputy's list for people who were more trouble than they were worth.

"It's kind of you to think of my grandfather," Wade finally said as he watched Barbara add the second layer of cake to the first. He wondered how much the Suttons owed their neighbors. He should have asked about his grandfather now and again over the years. It wouldn't have hurt him to send the old man a tin of cookies at Christmas, either. Maybe then he wouldn't need one of the church baskets. Of course, he'd still be shooting out those lights.

"I don't suppose Elmer could just take down his cross?" Wade asked.

"It's almost Christmas," Edith said, aghast. "We can't ask someone to take down their cross on the birthday of our Lord and Savior."

Wade nodded. He could see where this was going. "I know, a man has a right to display religious items on his own property, but—"

"Well, you can take away your grandfather's gun. That will solve it. He's caused enough trouble with that old thing. He shouldn't have it anymore anyway. Not in his condition," Edith added.

Wade couldn't argue with that. A drunkard had no business being armed. "He's probably just worried about coyotes getting to his livestock."

"The only animals he has left are a few chickens and that donkey of his," the sheriff said. "No coyotes will get inside the barn with that donkey there. She's mean enough to take care of a whole pack of them."

Wade felt his heart lift. "Jenny? He's still got Jenny?"

The sheriff nodded. "Don't ask me why. She bites anyone who goes near her."

Wade smiled.

"I forgot about the donkey," Edith said with a

light in her eyes. "We still don't have one this year for the pageant. Maybe—"

"That thing bites," the sheriff reminded everyone.

"Not around Christmas," Wade said. She did throughout the rest of the year, but somehow Jenny seemed to know what time of the year it was. She'd even let him rub her ears while he hid out in the barn over the holiday.

"The cake's ready," Barbara said as she finished sprinkling coconut on top of the frosting. "When the kids and Charley get back, we'll be all ready to eat dinner."

Just then, Wade heard footsteps on the back steps leading to the kitchen door. Everyone had returned. Barbara started gesturing for everyone to go into the dining room.

An hour later, Jasmine put her knife across the top of her dinner plate. "Everything was delicious."

They were all gathered in the dining room. They'd just eaten a roasted pork loin with sweet potatoes and glazed carrots. Barbara had made wheat dinner rolls and opened a small jar of rhubarb jam. It had been a feast.

"I haven't eaten food like that in a long time," Wade said from the other side of the table. "How'd you get everything to taste so good?"

Barbara smiled. "I was able to store the carrots and sweet potatoes from my garden. I think people can tell the difference between those and the ones I get in the store."

"Absolutely," Jasmine agreed as she looked around. If she didn't know better, she would think they were all posing for a Norman Rockwell painting. Everyone sat there with satisfied smiles on their faces and the empty serving platters in front of them showing what bounty they'd had to eat. Barbara had made a centerpiece of candles, pinecones and red berries. She'd even covered the table with an antique lace cloth.

This, Jasmine thought to herself, was what a holiday meal in a home should be like. She was learning to cook, but she realized that was only half of it. A family needed a home, too. She would find it easier to rebuild a tractor engine than to create a home like this. She didn't know what it was about her months in Dry Creek that made her long for a life like she saw in her friends here, but she wanted it badly.

Across the table, she saw Wade move slightly and she looked up at him.

"Oh." If she wasn't mistaken, she glimpsed the same longing in his eyes that she knew was in her own.

Wade gave her a little smile. "Beats frozen dinners, doesn't it?"

Jasmine nodded as her heart sank. A man like Wade would want home-cooked meals if he went to the trouble of getting married. She couldn't bake bread, either, she reminded herself. As for that cake their hostess was carrying to the table, it was pure fantasy to think she could ever do something like that.

The phone in the kitchen rang and the sheriff pushed back his chair.

"Our answer machine is broken," he said as he stood up. "But I'll ask them to call later so I'll be back before the cake's all dished up."

Jasmine watched as Barbara repeatedly slipped the knife into the cake. Then the woman lifted each slice up and slid it onto delicate china plates. The raspberry filling was so red it matched the berries in the centerpiece on the table.

Then the sheriff opened the door from the kitchen.

"Wade," he called. "Come here a minute."

Jasmine couldn't imagine what would require both men's attention when they'd been looking forward to the cake. Then she heard a single word before the sheriff completely closed the door behind them.

"Lonnie," the sheriff had said.

Jasmine looked around her. No one else seemed to react to the name. They must not know.

"Excuse me," she said as she stood. "I'll be right back."

Jasmine felt a tremor in her stomach. Something was wrong and she had a feeling it might be related to her.

Chapter Five

Jasmine put her shoulder to the kitchen door to push it open. She wondered if Lonnie had sent another postcard and the mailman was calling to warn the sheriff. It didn't seem likely the mailman would do that, but what else could it be? Maybe someone else had picked the postcard up from the counter in the hardware store and just now realized it?

"Excuse me, I—" Jasmine repeated as she opened the door.

The sheriff and Wade stopped talking and turned to look at her.

Jasmine stepped through the doorway and let the door close behind her. It was something worse than the postcard. She could tell because both men had changed from dinner companions to lawmen. They had that look in their eyes.

"I thought I heard you mention Lonnie," she said quietly as she squared her shoulders. She wasn't afraid to face her past. She'd been such a confused young woman. All the men she'd ever known had been losers like her mother's boyfriends. Lonnie hadn't seemed too bad at the time. She'd spent years paying for her foolishness in following Lonnie around, and if she had to pay more she would. It just made her realize how much of a dream it was to think she could erase her past and have a normal life where she got married and grew a garden or made centerpieces out of pinecones. She wondered if women like Edith and Barbara knew how fortunate they were.

"Do you know what he has planned?" Wade spoke first, his voice hard.

"Lonnie?"

Wade nodded. "Is he coming here?"

"What do you mean? He's in prison."

The sheriff cleared his throat. Jasmine looked at him and saw the sympathy in his eyes. "Lonnie escaped a few hours ago. The prison officials saw the pamphlet you sent him in his cell and they remembered the call I'd made checking on him. It seems he marked up that pamphlet a fair amount. Especially the part about the streets of gold and the city on a hill with a cross."

"Lonnie escaped?" Jasmine felt dizzy. "How could that happen?"

"He had to have had outside help," Wade said. His voice was even, but she could hear the condemnation in it.

It took her a moment to realize what he was thinking. "Well, it wasn't me. I was out there having dinner with all of you."

Wade nodded. "Which seems very convenient."

The counselors in prison had warned her that this might happen. She'd been prepared for people to look at her and only see her past. But that was before she'd found a place in Dry Creek. She'd let down her guard. No one here treated her like an ex-con. She'd become a child of God.

She looked at the sheriff. "Are you planning to arrest me?"

"Of course not," he said with an irritated glance over at Wade. "We just need to know if you can tell us anything about where Lonnie might go. I mean, he's been in jail for a long time. Why did he pick now to escape?"

Jasmine shrugged. "I have no idea. And I don't know where he'd go. Probably the closest place he could find to hide. He's not much of an outdoorsman, so I'd guess a big city. He likes to play pool and he does that to hustle up money when he's broke."

"I'll pass that along," the sheriff said. "In the meantime, we'll have to assign you some protection. Just in case he plans to head this way. The Feds will be here tomorrow to nose around, but in the meantime Wade will keep an eye on you."

A lump was starting to settle in her stomach. She looked up at Wade. "I don't want to put you out."

"No trouble," he said. He'd shaved since this morning, but his face was still grim. His jaw was tense. "I need to keep track of my grandfather now anyway. Since you're both out there, it'll be fine. I'll be around in case anyone stops by."

She wasn't fooled. Lawmen wouldn't be worried about Lonnie just coming by for a social visit. They'd be worried about her helping him. "Am I under house arrest, too?"

"I wouldn't call it that," the sheriff mumbled, but he looked embarrassed enough that she knew that's exactly what a judge would call it.

"Well." She turned to Wade and blinked. She willed herself not to cry. "I guess it's a good thing you're taking me home tonight, then. So you'll know exactly where I am. I suppose you'll want the keys to my motorcycle, too."

"It's for your own protection," the sheriff hurried to say.

Jasmine nodded. She felt real protected, all right.

They were quiet for a minute. Then the sheriff cleared his throat. "Barbara will be expecting us back for the cake."

No one moved.

"Are you going to tell them?" Jasmine asked, keeping her voice cool. She hadn't realized how bad this situation would feel until the sheriff mentioned the cake. How could she face everyone if they knew what the two men suspected?

The sheriff looked over at Wade.

"I don't see any need to do that," Wade said. He paused and looked right at her. "This might all blow over and no one would ever need to know."

Was that pity she saw in his eyes, Jasmine wondered. She hadn't let one tear escape. He didn't need to feel sorry for her.

"It's just routine," Wade added as he ran his fingers over his hair. Then he looked down. "Policy."

Jasmine nodded. They might as well give her an orange jumpsuit and a number.

"You'll still be able to move around." Wade cleared his throat and looked back at her. "Anywhere local, that is. I can drive you."

"Escort you," the sheriff corrected the other man. "You'll be escorting Miss Hunter."

Wade gave her what would pass for a smile if a person didn't pay too much attention. "That's right. Just let me know if you need to leave your father's place."

Jasmine forced herself to look up at him. His green eyes had darkened. The friendliness he'd shown in her father's kitchen was gone.

"I need to go over to your grandfather's tomorrow morning for the Covered Dish thing," she finally said.

"Well, that's fine, too." Wade's voice was professional. "I'll be around to give you a lift."

Jasmine stopped herself from asking how he'd prevent it if she wanted to run away. With her motorcycle, she could drive across the fields and slip through a fence past the gully east of her father's farm. Wade wouldn't even see her if he was watching the lane or the main road. And, if he did see her, that bike of hers could go where his car couldn't. She would be riding free, just like she'd been when she rode into Dry Creek last fall.

She had a spare key for her bike and, for a moment, the thought of leaving was tempting. But where would she ever find a place like this again? She couldn't run and build a home for herself at the same time. She had a chance for a new life here. She had the church. She had friends. At least, she hoped she had friends. She didn't know what would happen when the suspicions spread. Would people here think she could help a criminal? Still be a criminal?

"Fine," she finally said. She never had been a coward. "I guess we should go have some of that cake."

Wade followed Jasmine and the sheriff back into the dining room. He wished he had never come back to Dry Creek. Or, if he had come back, he wished people hadn't been so kind to him. Barbara making that cake for him was putting him off his game. And then Jasmine—usually, he didn't have any trouble taking a tough line with a suspect. But then he'd never been tempted to kiss a suspect before.

He watched Jasmine's back as she walked to the table. She was ramrod straight and angry with him. He knew he'd come on too strong, but it was either that or forgetting everything he knew about law enforcement and refusing to believe she could be responsible for anything.

As a lawman he had to consider all of the possibilities and it was hard to forget that Lonnie had been her partner. She could have sent him a coded message that helped him escape in some way, or at least given him an incentive to risk everything to get outside. Those streets of gold bothered him. Were they planning another robbery? Even the roll of bills the sheriff was flashing around this morning would be enough to tempt most criminals.

He wished he knew how to look into the heart of a person so he would know what Jasmine was thinking. Was she as innocent as she looked or as guilty as she'd been the first time she was convicted of a crime? He knew better than most how many ex-cons fell back into theft. He was often the one who took them in the second time around and listened to their sorry excuses.

"I gave you the biggest piece of cake," Barbara said as he sat down at the table.

"Thank you," Wade smiled. It was the cake of his childhood fantasies and he was going to have to force himself to eat it. All he wanted to do was take Jasmine home and then park his car at the end of the lane of her father's place. Why did she have to be tied up with Lonnie? Why couldn't she be a nice, ordinary woman like Barbara here? Carl never had to worry about arresting her.

Wade felt the smoothness of the cake on his

tongue and tasted the sweet tang of the raspberry filling. He smiled up at Barbara and thanked her again for the cake. The two kids at the table were smacking their lips and demanding more, just like Wade would be doing if he wasn't so troubled.

Then he looked down the table and saw his dear friend, Edith. She wouldn't be happy about him keeping an eye on anyone. It was clear the older woman was very fond of Jasmine. That, of course, was the problem with being a lawman and trying to have friends. He liked things black and white with no shades of gray. He didn't want to have feelings for the suspect.

By doing his job, he was going to upset Jasmine and everyone else in Dry Creek. For the first time since he'd driven into town, he missed the barren feel of his apartment in Idaho Falls. He knew who he was there.

It didn't take long for Wade to leave the Walls' house with Jasmine walking in front of him. The night was cold. Jasmine wrapped her arms around herself to keep warm and hurried to his car. He was still nursing that leg of his so he moved slower than she did. He made it in good time, though, and, as he opened the car door for her, she nodded her thanks and slid into the passenger seat.

The first thing Wade did after he got into the car

was to move the dial up on the heater. Snowflakes were just starting to fall, but they were scattered enough that he could clear them away with his windshield wipers.

He silently turned his car around and started down the sheriff's lane. The car lights shone on the falling snow, making the flakes look like pinpricks in the darkness. The black shapes of trees lined the rutted lane. It reminded him of stars and that led to thinking about angels, or at least one particular angel.

"I suppose you have to practice for the pageant," Wade finally said when they turned onto the main gravel road. His passenger was squeezed so close to the other door that she would almost disappear in the shadows if it wasn't for her red hair.

"We do it during the Sunday school time," she mumbled without looking over at him. "I can't miss practice. The pageant is on Christmas Eve."

It was Friday night. If the pageant was on Christmas Eve, that meant it was Monday night. Three days away. A lot of escaped prisoners were caught within the first forty-eight hours. Hopefully, everything would be back to normal by the time of the performance since that big barn would be hard to secure at night.

"No one's suggesting that you miss anything."

Wade tried to keep his voice friendly, hoping Jasmine would smile a little and ease the knot in his stomach.

Then, just like that, he knew what he could offer to her. "I'll be happy to help you practice for the pageant."

Even in the darkness, he could see her look over at him in surprise.

"You won't want to do the angel swing the way I did," he continued as he steered his car around a low point in the road. "But I can help with your flight angle and things. Some people end up hanging in the air like a sack of potatoes. You'll want to look like you're really flying."

"I changed my mind," Jasmine snapped back. She might be hiding in the shadows, but her voice was strong. "I don't need your help, after all."

The inside of the car was warm by now and Wade lowered the temperature dial. The snow had picked up speed and more flakes were flying.

Wade nodded and looked over at Jasmine. "That's fair enough. It's been years since I was in the pageant anyway. They probably do it different now."

She was silent for a minute. "It's the same story as always."

"I suppose."

"Timeless," she added.

"No doubt."

She was quiet for a bit longer then she spoke. "Oh, all right, you can help."

Wade wanted to smile, but he didn't. "I don't want to put you out any."

Heavy, wet flakes gathered on his windshield and he started the wipers again.

"If you must know, I could really use the help," Jasmine finally admitted. "Edith has lots of suggestions, but she's never done the flight and I want it all to be spectacular."

"Who has been doing the part until you showed up?"

"They put the angel on hold years ago until they finished the new wheel and rope thing. As I understand it, they've just been using a broadcast system for the 'Fear not' speech. Apparently, it wasn't very effective."

"I wouldn't think it would be," he agreed. "The shepherds need some help in looking awestruck."

"I want them to look happy."

Wade shrugged. "That's one way to go."

He had to admit the young boys who played the shepherd role were probably happier to see Jasmine as the angel than the shepherds had been when it was him in the role. He'd been only slightly older than most of them and they refused to gaze up at him in rapt adoration.

"What'd you do?" Jasmine asked.

Wade was glad he had her attention. "Trade secrets?"

He could see her nod.

"The only way I could think of to get the right expression on their faces was to throw dimes down on them," Wade admitted. "Everyone loves money and a dime bought a lot back then. I thought they'd look ecstatic."

"You did it when you were overhead?"

Wade shrugged. "I figured the dimes would sparkle on the way down and give a special effect. All their silver shiny surfaces."

Jasmine gave a small smile. "That's a great idea."

"I had the dimes in a bag attached to my leg," Wade explained. He was glad she was thawing. "I went over it a million times in my mind. But, when I was up there swinging, I had trouble getting the bag undone and—"

"Don't tell me you couldn't get it off your leg in time?"

"Worse. I got the bag untied from my leg, but it didn't open right and I was pulling on it in panic and—" He paused. "The bag fell on Alan Perkin's head and it had all those dimes in it. Almost made him pass out."

"Oh."

"It did make the shepherds look up into the sky with fear on their faces, though," Wade said as he heard her chuckle. "And Alan got to keep the dimes so he was okay with it. His mom was mad, but he wanted to get hit again. He was saving up for a new bike."

She was grinning now. "I've been thinking of using a couple of those Fourth of July sparklers. I figure if I tie them to my feet, they'll trail behind me."

Wade knew he had met his match. "They'd look like little stars."

"Exactly," Jasmine said with enthusiasm. "A whole galaxy of them."

Wade nodded. "Just be sure you have the paramedics there. I wish I'd thought that far ahead with Alan."

Jasmine was silent for a bit. "But Dry Creek doesn't have any paramedics. Charley works as a vet some, but—"

"The sheriff can get a paramedic unit to come down from Miles City if we need one. He's entitled to some of the county budget on that."

Wade figured the sheriff owned him one. "Maybe he should put the fire department on call, too."

Jasmine looked at him closely. "You're joking, right?"

Wade smiled. "All I can tell you is that I messed the whole angel thing up so bad that folks probably were thinking of calling out the National Guard. Alan was down there, almost passed out on the floor, and the other guys were scrambling around trying to get the dimes. And me, up there knowing I only had one chance at it. I gave a blood-curdling Tarzan yell and swung on that rope like a monkey in the jungle."

"Wow," Jasmine said.

"No one was even looking at the baby Jesus," Wade said. "And people cleared out of the barn before the kids had a chance to sing 'Silent Night.'"

"We're singing that, too."

"I think they sing it every year. It's the last thing as the shepherds and the wise men are looking down at the baby."

Wade turned the car into the lane of Elmer's place. He was glad Jasmine had loosened up around him. It didn't make her more or less guilty, but he felt better knowing she wasn't all knotted up inside. He told himself he would have put as much effort into seeing that any prisoner was at ease, but he knew it wasn't true. Usually, he didn't even talk as he brought someone in. He certainly didn't care if they were in any emotional distress. They were the bad guys; they deserved to suffer.

Wade was parking the car by the house when Jasmine turned to him.

"You're going to want to tell the Feds about my father's cars," she said to him. "He's got about four classics inside the barn that are worth big bucks. There's the Cadillac, a Bentley and a couple of early Fords."

Wade looked toward the big shape to his left. In the night, the barn looked black. "When you say big bucks—"

"I mean, they're worth stealing. I've started helping him restore them, but there's not as much work as I thought there'd be. He's kept them in mint condition. They're almost collection ready. I'd guess he could get a couple of hundred thousand for the lot of them."

Wade shut off the ignition. He'd never had a suspect confess before any crime had been committed. He didn't want Jasmine to put herself in jeopardy, though. "I'll mention it to the Feds, but I won't tell them you know how much the cars are worth."

Jasmine shrugged. "There's no reason for me to steal them anyway."

"It would be theft if you cheated him out of them, too."

"That's not what I meant," she said as she crossed her arms. "My father has offered me the cars repeatedly. He's put me in the will to get everything he owns if he dies. He'd like nothing better than for me to take his beloved cars."

Wade had indigestion. He hadn't even considered how much Elmer had that would pass to his natural daughter, especially if he assigned everything to her in his will. His farmland would be worth a few hundred thousand dollars, too. The streets of gold ended right in the middle of the old man's driveway. Wade hadn't even considered a potential murder in all of this.

"Does Lonnie know about your father?" Wade asked quietly.

Jasmine shook her head and then thought a minute. "Well, he might have known the three names I came to investigate. My mother didn't talk about her affairs. I didn't even know which one of the three men was my father when I knew Lonnie. But my mother had a box of journals and he might have read them. That's where I found the name of Edith's late husband and decided he was my father.

But the other two names were there, as well. I didn't even know then who my real father was."

Wade nodded. With the help of the Internet, Lonnie could have found out that Elmer was the only one of the three who was alive.

"You don't think Lonnie would do something to my father, do you?" Jasmine asked. She looked up at him with eyes full of worry. "Lonnie's not very stable. I wouldn't want anyone around here to be hurt by him."

Wade shrugged. "With all you'd inherit if Elmer were out of the picture—"

Jasmine gasped. "I don't care about the money."

"Lonnie might."

That turned her quiet. He didn't want her to worry.

"He won't even have the chance to get close to anyone," Wade assured her. "We'll have the Feds all over the place by tomorrow. Lonnie has a better chance of breaking into Fort Knox than he has of sneaking into Dry Creek."

Wade hoped he wasn't lying. He had no idea what the Feds would do. And, they might have some completely different theories as to why Lonnie had broken out of prison. It might have nothing at all to do with Jasmine or anyone in Dry Creek.

"You'll be safe," Wade said as he opened his door. He walked around to the passenger door and opened it. Jasmine stepped out of the car just as he realized he'd left her alone in the car with a loaded gun in the glove compartment.

Wade stood by the open car door and watched as Jasmine pulled her coat closer to her body. She wasn't making any move to walk toward the house and he wasn't making any move to let her. Finally, Wade reached up and touched her cheek. It was soft and a little damp. She must have been crying when she'd been huddled against the door on the drive out here.

"It'll be okay," he whispered to her as he brought his hand down.

"I'm fine," she said.

He nodded with a slight smile. "I know."

Wade had never kissed a suspect, but he would do it now if he didn't think it would make Jasmine cry even more. She was barely hanging on and he needed to leave her with her dignity.

"I'll be parked at the end of Elmer's lane if you need me," Wade said as he stepped back from the door. Snow was falling in earnest now, but he had a heavy sleeping bag in his trunk that he used on stakeouts like this. "I'll come to the door in the morning, before I go over to my grandfather's."

"You can't sleep outside all night. It's freezing

out here. I'll leave the kitchen door unlocked if you need to come inside."

"Don't leave anything unlocked. I'll duck into the barn if I need to."

Jasmine nodded.

Wade watched her walk to the kitchen door and go inside the house. Only then did he head back to the driver's door. He wondered if he'd get any sleep tonight. The next thing he knew he was going to be offering pillows to everyone he arrested and wishing them sweet dreams. When had he turned into a soft touch?

He waited for the light to go out in the kitchen before he started his drive down the lane. He already felt lonely.

Chapter Six

Jasmine stood on the cold wood floor of her bedroom and shivered as she buttoned up her bright yellow blouse. It was six o'clock and the gray morning light was just starting to seep through the blinds.

She'd stood at her closet door for a few minutes before deciding she needed something more powerful than the washed-out colors she'd worn lately. She'd been trying to blend in with the other women in Dry Creek, but the discouraging fact was that she was different. She couldn't be like the other women. Once an ex-con, always an ex-con. From now on she was wearing her boots.

She wasn't going to let Wade get her down, either. He might suspect she was planning the crime of the century. He might even think she was foolish enough to help Lonnie escape from the cell where he belonged. But he couldn't prove anything because it wasn't true. If she had to, she'd fight to clear her name of any suspicion.

After all, she was going to be the angel on Christmas Eve and she wanted people to watch her with a clear mind instead of worrying that she was going to steal their watches the minute their heads were bowed in prayer. Not that they would even think such a thing if Wade weren't around to spread rumors.

In her indignation, she wrestled a little too much with her buttons and tore one of them off her blouse. She went ahead and pinned the gap it left, but it looked kind of puckered so she put on her loose gray sweater so the blouse wouldn't show so much.

She looked odd when she saw herself in the mirror, but she defiantly went downstairs to the kitchen anyway. The day would have to take her as she was; she was tired of trying to change to please other people.

Ten minutes later, Wade was knocking at the back door. She knew it was him because she'd looked out the kitchen window earlier and watched his car slowly coming up the lane. It had snowed during the night and everything was white outside. Her father was in the barn doing his morning chores so she figured it was as good a time as any for Wade to appear. She hadn't figured out how to tell her father that she was being watched so she hoped Wade didn't come to the door with handcuffs or anything like that.

She was cooking and decided to strain the water from her pan of noodles before she made any move to answer the door. Wade could wait. She was getting ready to sprinkle the packet of dry cheese so she didn't want the noodles to sit in the water when they didn't have to. She wasn't much of a cook, but she had heard that most people let their pasta boil too long. She wasn't sure the noodles in the box of macaroni and cheese were that sensitive, but she was determined to do her best.

Besides, Wade was only here to stop her from breaking any laws, she told herself as she walked over to let him in.

"Cooking yourself breakfast?" Wade asked when she opened the door.

"Not yet." For the first time, Jasmine realized how much steam had been caused by boiling water for the noodles. The air coming in from the outside was frigid and immediately everything felt moist, even her face.

Wade's face went from white to pink as the

damp air settled over him. His hat had a dusting of snow on it and his coat collar was turned up to protect his neck.

She stepped aside so he could enter. "Cold out there?"

"I'm an icicle," Wade said as he stepped inside to the mat. He turned and closed the door behind him. Then he pulled his gloves off and started to rub his hands. "I thought my nose would freeze."

"Well, you could have come and knocked on the door," she scolded before realizing that, of course, he wouldn't. "I guess it would have compromised your honor, or whatever it is you lawmen have."

He took his hat off. "I didn't want to trouble you."

If he didn't want to trouble her, he shouldn't look the way he did. The cold made his jaw stand out more than normal. He needed a shave and his eyes were bloodshot. But, even with all that, he looked like a young boy just in from a snowball fight. It was clear he'd enjoyed being out in the cold. He wiped away the few flakes of snow still on his face but, when he'd done all that, he smiled.

"I'm going to fix some coffee soon." She would have offered to fix him a banquet if she had known how his eyes would light up. "You'll be welcome to some."

"Sounds great."

She nodded. Nobody could make better coffee than her, even if everything else was up for grabs.

"It'll be a few minutes," Jasmine said as she turned to walk back to the stove. "I'm in the middle of baking something."

That might have been too optimistic of a statement, but she let it stand.

It wasn't until Jasmine got back to the stove that she realized she'd be more comfortable if Wade wasn't there to watch her make her version of macaroni and cheese. Especially because the cooked noodles had turned hard and crusty in the few minutes that she'd left them uncovered. And the dry cheese mixture looked like sawdust as she tried to stir it in.

"Smells good," Wade said from where he patiently stood by the door. He had his hat in his hands as snow melted off his boots onto the mat.

She looked over at him. "You can't possibly smell anything. Besides, the noodles are stuck to the bottom."

She took the pan off the stove and tilted it so she could scrape it better. "I don't know what's wrong."

That statement pretty much summed up her life of late, she thought. Everything was supposed to be getting better since she'd become a Christian.

Instead, it felt like it was going backward. She couldn't believe someone standing right here in her kitchen thought she might still be a criminal.

She set the pan back down on the stove in defeat.

"Try adding some boiling water," Wade said, and then he hesitated. "Not that I'm any expert on cooking. Usually—"

"I know. Usually, its women that are supposed to be the experts," she snapped back at him. "But not all women know how to cook. It's not something that we're born knowing. Some of us have outside lives, too."

She shouldn't have to spell out that her outside life had been lived behind walls for the past few years.

He looked at her cautiously. "I was going to say I usually eat out."

"Oh. Well."

"I only mentioned the boiling water because I know it sometimes works with things that are glued together. Not that I think your noodles are glued. I'm sure they're good."

Jasmine nodded. "Thanks."

She kept her head down and her hands moving. She really should have made her coffee before she started on the casserole for Wade's grandfather. It seemed she was a little irritable without her cup of brew. Of course, she did have some extra stress.

She was the newest member of the Covered Dish group at church and this was the first dish she'd made for anyone. If she hadn't been determined to join every single group the church had, she wouldn't be part of this one anyway.

"If all else fails, you're welcome to the crackers I have in my trunk," Wade said. "They're better with butter, but—"

Somehow, in the time she'd been looking down at the mess of noodles, Wade had moved closer. He'd taken his boots off and left them by the door. He wore thick gray stockings and one of them was unraveling around the big toe.

"Butter. That's what I need," she said as she looked up. "That's what I forgot—that and the milk. It doesn't take much, but it makes the cheese work."

Jasmine set the pan back on the stove. The refrigerator was just five steps away, but she was feeling a little flustered and couldn't seem to move. "Do you always loom over your prisoners like this?"

Wade was standing so close she could count the whiskers on his chin. He stepped back in surprise. "You're not my prisoner. I'm protecting you."

She stepped to the refrigerator and opened the door. "I don't think anyone camps out in freezing temperatures because they're protecting someone."

"I do," he said quietly.

"Yeah, well," she muttered as she grabbed a cube of butter and the carton of milk. "Lonnie isn't coming here. He doesn't even know how to get here." She saw the doubt race across his face. "I know I could have told him how to find me, but I didn't. You're just going to have to trust me on that."

She wasn't looking at him, but she knew if she looked up she would see an expression of incredulity on his face. A lawman could never trust an ex-con, not entirely. She turned to the stove so she wouldn't have any chance of seeing him. "Now, if you'll excuse me, I have some cooking to do."

She was glad he didn't say anything.

Even though he wasn't wearing his boots, she could hear him slowly walk over to the table and sit down in one of the chairs.

"That leg of yours bothering you?" she asked.

"Not too bad," he said. "I was able to stretch out in the car."

"I'll get to that coffee in a second." She felt a little bad about snapping at him earlier. Even if he didn't need to guard her lane, he'd been uncomfortable doing it.

"Don't worry about me."

"I'm not worried." She looked up and there he

was waiting patiently again. "I'm just being hospitable."

He smiled then. A long, lazy smile that made the morning feel warmer even though the sky outside was still gray. "Actually, I thought maybe I could take you to breakfast at the café instead. After we go over and check on my grandfather."

Jasmine felt her spirits rise.

Then he added. "I need to meet up with the Feds anyway and I can't leave you out here alone until we figure out what's going on."

"Oh," she said as she dumped the macaroni and cheese into a small glass dish. So, that was it. "I wouldn't be alone. My father is here."

"I forgot about Elmer," Wade said with a frown. "He'll have to come with us, too. I can't leave him out here alone, either."

Jasmine put the lid on the dish and squared her shoulders. "He usually goes into Dry Creek when he finishes his chores anyway. He sits in the hardware store with the other guys and drinks his coffee while they all sit around that old woodstove. On a day like today, they'll stay there until noon."

"That sounds safe enough."

"We may as well leave then," Jasmine said.

She had to walk out to the barn, of course, to tell her father that she was going over to the Sutton place with Wade and then into Dry Creek. And Wade had to walk with her because he considered it his duty. At least he didn't say anything.

"You and Wade?" her father had asked when she stepped inside the barn and relayed her message. Fortunately, the man in question was giving her some room and was standing a few yards outside the barn door.

"It's just—" Jasmine started, and then trailed off.

"You don't need to explain," her father said as he grinned. "I know you young people like to spend time getting to know each other."

"It's not like that," Jasmine said in dismay. "We don't want to know each other."

Her father chuckled. "I remember when I was courting. No man comes out this early in the morning—after driving you to dinner the night before—unless he's got courting on his mind. Especially not in the snow."

"Trust me. Wade Sutton is not dating me," she said. "And I think he likes the snow."

Her father just kept smiling. "Wait until Charley hears this. He'll have to put a bug in his nephew's ear if he hopes to step up to the plate."

"Conrad's my boss," Jasmine protested. "You can't say anything like that."

She wondered when the people of Dry Creek decided she was fated to be with Conrad.

"Why? Lots of women marry their bosses."

"I don't," Jasmine said firmly. She hadn't thought any more about it since Edith had mentioned it, but she just didn't think Conrad was meant for her. Oh, he was nice enough—really nice, actually—and… The thought struck her out of nowhere and almost brought her to her knees. She thought Conrad was too nice for her. That couldn't be good, could it? Shouldn't she want to marry the nicest man in the world?

"It wouldn't do any harm for your young man out there to think you might be interested in Conrad, though," her father said as he walked closer to the barn door and peered out. "Men like a little competition."

Wade certainly wasn't the nicest man in the world. He was opinionated and exasperating and distrustful. Besides, she'd promised herself long ago she'd never become involved with a man who used a gun again, no matter which side of the law he was on.

"This is not a competition. Besides—" Jasmine started, but her father stepped out the door and away from her.

Oh, dear, as if she didn't have enough on her

mind, she was going to have to go out there and make sure her father didn't embarrass her completely. She waited a minute first on the off chance that her father would come to his senses and return before she had to look like a fool racing after him. She already looked incompetent in front of Wade and she didn't want to add to the list he was probably keeping of her shortcomings.

Chapter Seven

Wade noticed that the Maynard barn needed a new coat of paint. And there were a few dead weeds gathered against its foundation. It wasn't the first time since he'd been back in this area that he had seen there was a lot of work to be done. The people here were getting old. And not enough men of his age were here to do the hard, physical work of farming.

The fields behind the barn didn't look like they'd been planted last year, either. He never drove anywhere in Idaho or Montana without noticing the fields at the sides of the road. Before his grandfather had run him and his father off the family farm, Wade had expected to live his life right there. He'd always liked to watch crops grow. Even now he missed the itch from the wheat shaft on his skin when harvest was in full swing.

Wade looked up when he saw Elmer walking out of the barn with a big grin on his face.

"Morning," the older man said. "It's good to see you up and around so early."

"Well, I just—" Wade started to explain.

"Don't say anything," Elmer interrupted him. "Jasmine told me all about it."

"She did?" Wade didn't know whether to be relieved or annoyed. It was rightly his job to tell Elmer about Lonnie escaping from jail. But if Jasmine had already done it, so be it. "I don't want you to worry. I've got it all under control."

Jasmine was walking toward them, her arms swinging in that way he'd first noticed out the café window. He wondered what was bothering her now. He couldn't help but wish she was still wearing a dress instead of her jeans and that heavy gray sweater that hung halfway to her knees. There was just something about the sway of a skirt when a woman walked like she did.

Elmer grunted as he looked over his shoulder at his approaching daughter. "A man always thinks that he's got it under control, but sometimes there's more going on than meets the eyes."

"Don't listen to him," Jasmine said when she

reached them. Her auburn hair was sticking up here and there and white puffs of air came out of her mouth when she spoke. He was surprised he hadn't noticed the generous curve of her mouth before; he could look at her all day. He forced himself to pay close attention as she continued. "Conrad is only my boss. All he cares about is whether or not I can get that combine engine fixed before it's time to harvest next year. It's in an 8780 and some widow up by Miles City is relying on it—"

"You're working on a *combine engine?*" Wade was stunned. And impressed. When people had said she worked in Conrad's mechanic shop, he thought she was the secretary or the bookkeeper.

"It's only temporary," Elmer jumped in, speaking quickly. "Until she gets married and settles down. And Conrad—"

Wade got it now. "I understand everyone wants her to marry this Conrad fellow. You don't need to worry. I should be finished with her before Christmas."

Elmer's mouth hung open. "Just like that."

"It's okay," Jasmine said as she took Elmer's arm. "It's not what you're thinking—"

"In my day, we did things differently," Elmer said with enough bluster in his voice to wake any chickens that were roosting on the place. "Men treated women with respect and—" All of a sudden he got a strange expression on his face and looked at Jasmine. "I never thought with your mother. I mean, I couldn't marry her because I was—I never thought—and then she had you and I didn't know—"

Elmer finally gave up and hung his head.

Wade felt like he should give the two some privacy, but he was rooted to the ground.

Jasmine gently put her hand on Elmer's shoulder. "My mother didn't have any hard feelings about you. At least, she never mentioned any."

Elmer looked up. "She'd have a thing or two to say to me if I didn't see you were respected, though. That's all I can do now to make up for any of it."

Then Elmer turned to glare at Wade. "You break my daughter's heart and I'll make you wish you hadn't. I don't care what kind of lawman you are."

Wade felt warm inside even though it was freezing outside. Elmer thought he had a chance. "I won't break anyone's heart."

He heard Jasmine draw in her breath as if she was going to say something, but he never dreamed she'd be so upset at what Elmer was thinking that she'd tell the truth.

"Wade has me under arrest," she said. Her voice

was clipped and empty of emotion. "There's nothing else going on here."

"What?" Elmer's eyes were starting to bulge.

Wade wondered if the older man was going to have a stroke.

"Now, that's not right," Wade said. "Protective custody would be a better way to say it."

"I don't care how you say it." Elmer found his voice. "This is still my land and you're not welcome here. I'll thank you to leave."

Wade nodded. He knew how Elmer felt. "It's for her own good. Her old partner escaped from jail and there's reason to believe he might come here."

"That no-account Lonnie?" Elmer asked. "How'd he get out of jail?"

"We don't know," Wade answered.

"They think I might have helped," Jasmine said quietly from where she stood beside Elmer.

"Well, that's nonsense," Elmer said as he turned to her. "Why would you help him? He's the one who got you locked up to begin with."

Jasmine smiled. "No, I'm the one who got me locked up. But, you're right, I have no reason to help Lonnie."

Elmer looked over at Wade before turning back to his daughter. "Well, I suppose he better stay around in case you need help, then. At least he has a gun."

"I'll do my best to protect you both," Wade promised.

Elmer grunted. "I can take care of myself. You worry about Jasmine."

Wade nodded. He understood how the man felt. "We don't even know if Lonnie is headed this way. Jasmine and I going into Dry Creek after we check on my grandfather. We need to meet up with the Feds and we may as well do it there."

Wade had his day planned out. He looked over at Jasmine. "Ready to go?"

She nodded and they walked toward his car.

Wade wished Jasmine would talk to him as they drove over to his grandfather's place. But she just sat there with her glass dish clutched in her hand. He didn't quite understand why she was taking her macaroni and cheese over to his grandfather, but he knew it had something to do with that Covered Dish group at church. Maybe they were trying to get the old man to eat his lunch instead of drink it.

The wooden gate that marked the entrance to his grandfather's farm was hanging crookedly from its hinges. The boards themselves were a weathered gray and splintered so badly they didn't look like they'd last much longer. Deep ruts in the lane spoke of neglect. No one had grated the road in decades. Beside the road, dead grass was rotting under the damp snow.

Wade slowed his car as he drove toward the house. He told himself he was giving his grandfather time to realize he had company coming, but he wasn't so sure he could have driven faster anyway.

The fields beside the lane hadn't been plowed in years. He looked farther out and saw the far field didn't look tended, either. With the proper care, a good crop always grew in that field, even when water was short. He wondered if his grandfather was farming at all. He could have at least leased the land on shares to someone.

"You need to park by the old pickup," Jasmine said as he got closer to the house. "That's as far as we can go."

"What are you talking about?" He turned to look at her.

"The Covered Dish group," she said. "That's as far as we're allowed to go. Edith got your grandfather to agree to that much. We just leave the food in the pickup and he comes and gets it."

"You mean, you do this often?" Wade was stunned. It wasn't just something for Christmas?

"Every other day," Jasmine said with a matter-of-fact nod. "We would do it every day, but Edith said we shouldn't push him."

"You shouldn't have to feed him," Wade said as he stopped his car beside the pickup. He looked around. The house looked almost deserted. There were no curtains on the windows and the paint was chipped off so much that the yellow boards had turned a sickly beige.

What had happened? His grandfather should be prosperous. He'd have his social security payments by now and he'd always talked about his investments. Was he just so drunk that he didn't care?

A figure moved in one of the windows and Wade's stomach clenched. His grandfather had seen them. Wade had to remind himself that he wasn't a boy any longer; he didn't have to worry about taking a beating from the old man inside the house.

Still, Wade thought as he looked over at Jasmine, it wasn't only his grandfather's fists that could be unpleasant. The old man had a tongue on him that was just as bad.

"Why don't you stay in the car here?" Wade said, trying to keep his voice casual. "Let me check on my grandfather and let him know I'll be keeping an eye on him and that shotgun of his."

Jasmine looked up at him and then nodded. "I'm sure you'd like some privacy."

Wade grunted. He wasn't expecting any heart-warming scene inside that house if that's what she meant. "I shouldn't be long."

Wade opened his car door.

"I'll pray for you," Jasmine said just as he started to close it.

That stopped him in midmotion. He bent down and looked inside his car at her. "Don't waste your breath. My grandfather is beyond all that."

Jasmine shrugged. "So was I. But Edith prayed for me anyway."

Wade knew better than to argue with her on this. "Well, do what you want. Just don't expect anything to happen because of it."

Wade stepped back and shut the door before she could say anything else. He knew better than most that God didn't answer people's prayers. He couldn't count the number of times he'd lain in bed at his grandfather's house and prayed for his father to return from prison or his mother to be raised from the dead. By then he knew God had done things like that before. He'd learned about it in Sunday school.

He shook his head. Sunday school just didn't match up with real life.

Wade forced himself to knock on his grandfa-ther's door. He wondered if the old man would even recognize him after all of these years. It might be best for them both if he didn't.

Wade had to wait for the door to open. He could hear the locks being pulled so he stood there and reminded himself he was an officer of the law. Sort of. He and the sheriff didn't have a formal agreement on this, but—

The door opened a crack.

"What d'ya want?" an old man's voice asked.

Wade tried to see inside, but all that was visible was an inch of face with one suspicious bloodshot eye squinting out at him.

"I've come back to—" Wade started to speak when the door opened fully and he stopped.

There was his grandfather. He used to be a giant of a man, but he had shrunk and he seemed to be mostly bone. His hair was almost gone and, what was left of it, was hanging in uneven strands. He was wearing a dingy T-shirt that used to be white and baggy jeans that were held in place by worn black suspenders.

"Sonny? Is that you?"

Wade's heart sank. What was wrong with the old man?

"It *is* you," his grandfather said with joy on his face. "I knew you'd come back someday."

Wade couldn't take it any longer. "Sonny's

dead. Remember he died in a shoot-out with the cops. Sonny was my father. I'm Wade."

It was silent on the porch.

Finally, his grandfather looked up at him in puzzlement. "That can't be right. You have to be Sonny. That nice woman you married is out in the car right now. I can see her. Don't know what I'd do without her. I knew you'd come back to see her, even if you didn't want to see me."

Wade stared at his grandfather. He knew the man wasn't joking; he didn't have a sense of humor. "Have you seen a doctor lately?"

"I don't need a doctor." His grandfather reared back and shouted. "I'm as healthy as a horse."

Wade heard a car door shut behind him and he looked around. Jasmine had gotten out of the car. She probably had heard the yell if nothing more.

"Do you need help?" she called.

"I don't know," he answered back as she kept walking forward.

"Have her come in," his grandfather said as he turned to go inside the house. "I haven't had a chance to visit with your wife for some time now."

"She's not—" Wade said as he followed his grandfather inside. Then he decided that was the least of the old man's worries. He glanced back and saw Jasmine still coming. He'd have to find a moment to clue her in to his grandfather's craziness.

When he turned around, he saw the kitchen counter.

"What in the world?" Wade couldn't believe it. Dozens of casserole dishes were spread all over the counter. Some yellow glass ones. A couple of metal ones. A few black ceramic ones. Red ones. Blue ones. "There must be twenty, maybe thirty, dishes here."

"Edith comes by and picks them up now and again," his grandfather said. "She'll be by soon. I wash them up for her."

Wade was relieved to see, as he stepped closer, that the dishes were at least all clean.

"She must take them to that wife of yours and she fills them up again," his grandfather said with a frown on his face. "I've never figured out that part of it."

"It's the women at the church," Wade said. "They're the ones who bring you the food."

His grandfather looked at him as if he was trying to remember something. "I don't think that could be right. I didn't figure anyone but your wife would do it anyway. She likes me okay, you know?"

Wade nodded. He did remember a time as a young child when his mother had been alive and this house had been happy. Maybe his mother had liked her father-in-law. The old man hadn't been drinking as much back then so he was probably easier to be around.

He looked over at his grandfather and saw him looking up quizzically.

"You should be nice to that wife of yours, son," he said. "She's what keeps this family together."

Wade nodded. He could hear Jasmine on the steps now. Somewhere inside him was a faint hope she would know what he needed to do. He had no idea his grandfather was this bad off. The old man obviously shouldn't be living out here by himself. He wouldn't fare well in one of those nursing homes, though. And, the idea of bringing his grandfather to his apartment in Idaho Falls was ludicrous, of course. What he needed to do was to find someone he could hire to move in and take care of his grandfather.

"Jasmine," Wade greeted her as she walked through the door into the kitchen.

"That's not her name," his grandfather said with a frown. "What is it? Patricia? No, Maria? It was something with an *a* at the end and it was a pretty name."

"Annabelle," Wade finally said. "Her name was Annabelle."

"That's right," his grandfather said in relief. "I knew it was on the tip of my tongue."

Wade nodded as he watched Jasmine look at them in bewilderment. He didn't even know how to explain to her that his confused grandfather was living in a world that had been gone for over thirty years.

Chapter Eight

Jasmine couldn't believe Mr. Sutton was smiling at her. Everything she had ever heard about the man led her to believe he'd greet her at the door with a shotgun instead of an invitation to come in and sit down.

"It's so nice to meet you," Jasmine said as she stepped farther into the kitchen. The old man began to chuckle. "Why you've known me for years."

The day was gray outside and the house was filled with shadows even though there were no curtains on the windows. She had to let her eyes adjust to the darkness. Then she looked up at Wade to see if he knew what his grandfather was talking about.

"My grandfather thinks you're my mother," Wade quietly said as he stepped closer so only she could hear.

"What?" Jasmine put her hands up to her hair. She might not look her best, but—

"And he thinks I am my father," Wade continued.

"Oh." Jasmine was silent for a moment. "That's why he's so friendly."

"Apparently," Wade said grimly. "He's discovered a love for his family at last."

Jasmine could feel the tension in Wade. She supposed he was disappointed that his grandfather didn't recognize him. She'd never had a grandparent, but she knew some children grew attached to them. And, of course, Wade had been raised by his.

"I'm sorry," she said.

Wade turned to his grandfather and raised his voice. "We need to be going. But I'll come back in a few hours."

"With your wife?" his grandfather asked.

"No, she won't be back."

Jasmine didn't like the disappointment she saw in the old man's eyes. She could visit again, but she didn't get her mouth opened soon enough to say so.

"But she has to come back," Wade's grandfather said, looking a little frantic. "This is her home. It's my fault, I suppose. I should have made you pay more attention to her. I'm your father. I knew it was important."

"It's okay," Wade said as he reached a hand out to put on his grandfather's arm.

"No, it's not okay," his grandfather thundered as he shook the hand off.

Jasmine stepped back. Now, this is the man she'd expected to meet when she walked up to the door of this house. Even in his sagging suspenders, the old man looked fierce.

"She doesn't care—" Wade started to say.

The old man glared at him. "Right here and now. I want you to kiss your wife and tell her that you have feelings for her. If I had made you do that more often, everything would be different."

"It's okay," Jasmine said as she made fluttery motions to the old man. "I'm fine. Really."

"Now, son," the old man said, his voice just as firm as it had been. "Do it now."

"No, I—" Jasmine looked up and saw that Wade had taken another step toward her.

"It's easier," Wade said softly as he bent his head to hers.

No, it wasn't easier, Jasmine thought as she felt his lips on hers. It was just as she had feared. Her heart started to beat faster. Her mind forgot to worry. Everything in her focused on the man kissing her. The man who didn't trust her. The man who—oh, my, she felt as if she was floating.

Everything was in slow motion, but she did her best to pull away from Wade. And then she noticed he looked a little stunned himself. His eyes held hers and wouldn't let go. So she stayed where she was, close enough that she could feel his breath on her face.

"I need to—" She started to say something and then forgot the excuse she'd been going to offer for moving away.

"I know," Wade answered anyway.

"Well, isn't that nice," the old man said in satisfaction as his gaze moved between the two of them. "I can see you're reminded of just how much you love each other."

That made Wade break away. "We're not—"

Jasmine stepped farther away, too. "We certainly are not— I'd never—"

"We need to leave," Wade finally said and he grabbed Jasmine's hand and guided her out of his grandfather's house.

The day hadn't gotten any warmer when they were in the Sutton house, but Jasmine was ready to fan her face even though it was forty degrees outside. What did she think she was doing, kissing a lawman that had more suspicions than he had feelings toward her?

"I'm sorry about that," Wade said as he walked

beside her to his car. "I didn't know what else to do and—"

His excuse trailed off.

She turned to him. "Edith will want those dishes back. I'm sure some women in the church are running out of baking pans completely."

There, she thought to herself as she opened the car door before he could reach for the handle. She wasn't about to let him know she'd been affected by that kiss, not when it had just been the easy way out for him. She watched him as he walked around the car to the driver's seat. She hoped his leg hurt him.

"I don't know how I'm going to thank everyone," Wade said when he slid into the driver's seat.

He sounded so miserable, Jasmine's heart softened. "Just the words would do."

Wade shook his head. "I didn't expect other people to take care of my grandfather. I honestly thought he was okay. Oh, I figured he was probably ornery as always. But I never dreamed he needed so much help. He probably would have stayed in that house and starved to death if it weren't for the church."

"Well, Edith does keep an eye on him. I thought she wrote you a letter a couple of months ago about your grandfather. She got the address from Carl."

"I don't always get all my mail," Wade said as he started the car.

Jasmine wished she had that problem. If she hadn't gotten that postcard, she wouldn't be sitting here in Wade's car right now. Better yet, if she hadn't sent Lonnie that pamphlet, he wouldn't have even written the postcard.

It would have been a pamphlet, though, because it had been a wonderful tract. She still remembered the words about how glorious heaven was with its streets of gold and the cross high on the hill. She'd wanted to give it to Lonnie because he liked shiny, gold things. And, if anyone needed God's grace more than she did, it was her old partner in crime.

The sadness of it all made her sigh.

"You have my full apology, of course," Wade said as he passed by the broken-down gate of his grandfather's farm and turned the car onto the main gravel road.

Jasmine looked up and saw the frown on his face.

"You can file a complaint," he continued. "Sheriff Wall should have a form."

It suddenly dawned on Jasmine. "Because of the *kiss?* You're worried because you kissed me when you were on duty?"

He turned and looked at her. "It's only fair that you know you have the option. I was out of line."

"Duly noted," she said.

They were both silent for a moment.

"Not that I regret it," Wade finally muttered, so low she could barely hear him.

Jasmine decided that Conrad was looking better all of the time. At least he didn't make her half-crazy like Wade did. Not that she would consider a man who used a gun to make his living anyway.

"Don't worry. I'm not filling out any form," she said.

"Thanks."

"I have better things to do."

They were silent as they continued into Dry Creek. About halfway there, Jasmine pulled a small mirror out of her purse and tried to make sense of her hair. She had a little tube of mousse in her purse and squirted some into her hands. It was too late to try for curls and she was more in the mood for the spiked look today anyway. That way people wouldn't be so likely to notice the bulky gray sweater that made her look like a refugee from a war zone.

"Nobody's going to take your picture today, if that's what you're worried about," Wade said finally.

Jasmine gasped and jerked up from her mirror. "I never thought about them taking a picture if they arrest me. Can they do that?"

"I meant the press," Wade said. "Sometimes a reporter will get a tip that the Feds are working on something and they'll come along to see what they can find."

"Well, I'm certainly not going to be talking to any reporters. I'm just hoping no one tells everyone that I'm suspected of doing anything."

"Sheriff Wall is very discreet."

Jasmine knew she was doomed. Oh, Carl may not say anything. But someone was going to say something if a carload of agents in suits pulled into Dry Creek. There was no way they'd blend in. And, if Wade insisted on dragging her all over with him, people were going to ask why.

"I don't suppose you can deputize me," she finally asked. "Just so people think I'm working when I'm with you."

He actually took his eyes off the road to stare at her. "I'm not even a deputy myself. I'm independent."

Fortunately, there was no traffic on the road. They hadn't passed another car the whole time Wade had been driving into town.

"It wouldn't need to be official or anything," she said. "I just don't want to stir up people's curiosity about why I'm with you. Maybe you could ask me to take notes or something."

She looked at him hopefully.

"I guess I couldn't stop you from taking notes," he said. Which was probably as much encouragement as she was going to get, she decided.

"Thanks."

Jasmine knew the Feds were in town the minute they turned the corner and could see the shiny black car parked at the café. None of the local cars were that clean, not in winter with all of the slush on the roads around town. Everyone would know strangers were here.

"I don't suppose you have a notebook?" Jasmine asked as Wade parked his car beside the federal one.

Wade looked at her and then leaned down to open his glove compartment. "I think I have one in here someplace."

His elbow dug into her knee as he rummaged around in the compartment. Finally, he pulled out a tattered green notebook and held it up triumphantly. It looked as if it'd been chewed up by a dog.

"That's the only one you have?" she asked. "It doesn't look very official."

"I don't take a lot of notes."

"I guess it will have to do, then." She accepted it from his hand.

"Knock yourself out." Wade moved back and

took the key out of the ignition. "Don't expect the Feds to say much in your presence, though."

Jasmine nodded.

When they stepped onto the café porch, she looked through the windows and saw three men sitting at a table. Wade saw them, too, and before he opened the door he turned and inspected her. She felt like a bug under a microscope. Then he reached up and flattened down her hair.

"Hey—" she protested.

"It's better without the spikes. Makes you look more innocent."

"I *am* innocent." Of course, now she probably looked like a drowned rat that didn't have the brainpower to help someone escape from prison. Maybe that was what Wade meant by innocent. That she was didn't look capable of committing a complex crime.

"And don't talk too much," he added. "Just smile. Answer all the questions truthfully, but don't volunteer anything extra."

"I don't know anything to volunteer. I didn't do anything."

"Yeah, well," Wade said and, with those encouraging words, he opened the door to the café.

All of the chitchat and silverware noise stopped the minute she stepped through the door. All three agents were dressed in black suits and looked ready for action. Fortunately, their eyes weren't focused on her.

"What took you so long?" they said to Wade in unison.

She turned around in time to see Wade shrug.

"Family business," he said.

She could see the shock on the faces of the agents. Finally, the man who looked the oldest in the group, cleared his throat.

"You've always said you didn't have any family," the man said. "What'd you do, Sutton? Get married?"

Now they all turned to look at her. Jasmine couldn't believe it. Here she was, with her hair plastered to her head and her blouse with a safety pin where a button should be, and they thought she was a bride. No wonder they were looking at her as if she had an extra eyeball in the middle of her forehead.

To make it worse, Wade just chuckled.

"Not yet," he said. "I'll let you know when we sign up."

The agents laughed a little, too, like it was a joke. Which she supposed it was, but it didn't do anything to help her self-esteem. She waited for Wade to mention his grandfather. Or at least say he was the one who had squashed her hair down like it was against the law to have a spike in place.

"Sit down and have some coffee," the older man offered.

"Just as soon as I get her settled," Wade said as he took hold of Jasmine's elbow and steered her to a table in the back of the café.

"But—" she started to say.

"They won't say anything with you at the table," Wade said. "Just order a pot of coffee and I'll be back in time to drink it with you."

"But—"

Wade nodded to the chair in front of her. "If you want to take notes, you can take them from here."

Now that would make her look like an idiot, Jasmine thought as she sat down. She wasn't that keen on hearing what the agents had to say anyway. Not if they were convinced she was involved.

She watched Wade walk back to the agent's table and saw the other men move their chairs so he'd have room to pull another one up beside them. She was surprised he knew these men. How many federal agents were there around anyway? She saw one of the agents slap Wade on the shoulder and she smiled.

Wasn't that nice? He had friends. She hadn't

realized that the men he worked with would be his family.

Just then Linda, the young woman who owned the café, came out of the kitchen and walked over. She wore a large bib apron over her jeans and T-shirt.

"Come in to see the sights?" Linda asked as she pulled an order pad out of her apron pocket. She nodded her head toward the agents. "It's not every day we see men coming to town in suits. We women need to enjoy it."

Jasmine tried to smile. "Do you know why they're here?"

Linda shrugged. "I figure they're IRS guys going out to the Elkton ranch. A big place like that gets audited now and again. Whoever they are, they sure look federal."

Jasmine knew she should tell the café owner that the men weren't here about the Elkton ranch. But she couldn't get the words past the lump in her throat. She was afraid she'd begin to cry if she started to explain.

"Want to start with a pot of coffee?" Linda asked.

Jasmine nodded and the café owner went off to get one.

One of the men at the other table laughed and Jasmine looked over. She wondered what they were saying. And what could possibly be funny in the situation. Since she could only hear snatches of their conversation, she did the only thing she could. She bowed her head and prayed God would smite them with the truth.

Thinking of them being brought low like the Philistines had been in the Old Testament, maybe with a few locusts thrown in for extra measure, brought a smile to her lips. She liked to remember that God had protected His children against overwhelming odds. He stood up for the oppressed. Three federal agents, who just needed to see the truth, would be nothing to Him.

Well, make that four, she thought with a broader smile. Wade needed to be convinced, as well. She'd give him an extra dose of locusts.

She'd no sooner gotten deep into prayer before the whole place went silent.

Chapter Nine

Wade almost groaned. He'd been telling the Feds his doubts that Jasmine had helped Lonnie escape when what did she do but close her eyes and start to smile like she was a fool with a secret. She couldn't have looked guiltier if she had pulled a gun out of her purse.

"What's she doing?" one of his buddies asked as he looked across the café.

That made the other two agents turn and stare.

"I think she's praying," Wade said.

There was silence.

"Most folks cry when they're praying," the agent commented suspiciously. "They don't smile like that."

"She doesn't have any food in front of her,

either," another one of them observed. "So she can't be saying grace or anything."

"People in this town pray a lot." Wade was tempted to close his eyes, too, just to avoid explaining it all. "Smiling, crying, food or no food—they do it all the time."

"Oh." The agents all turned their heads back to their table.

"You were saying you don't think she meant to send Lonnie the postcard?" one of the agents picked up the discussion they'd been having.

"Oh, she meant to send it," Wade clarified, relieved that everyone had stopped staring at Jasmine. "I just don't think she meant for it to say anything. It was an act of religious devotion."

If they were talking about any other suspect, Wade would be amused. His colleagues all started to frown. They weren't exactly comfortable trying to judge a person's religious sincerity. Neither was he when it came to that.

Fortunately, he'd grown up in this small town and knew a good number of people here believed in God and prayer with everything they had inside themselves. He hadn't envied anyone for a long time, but last night he had started to feel wistful when Edith had blessed the food. It would be nice to believe God cared as much as she thought He did.

"Here's a copy of what Ms. Hunter sent," the agent on his right said as he handed a photocopied sheet to Wade. "The original is at the lab being tested."

Wade accepted the copy of the pamphlet Jasmine had mailed off. He might even read it tonight, he told himself. He hadn't given much thought to heaven lately.

"They're still working on how Lonnie got out," the man continued. "Another inmate went with him."

This was the first time Wade had heard about that. "Well, maybe it was the other guy that had a contact on the outside, then."

"Maybe," the agent agreed with a shrug. "We don't know at this point."

"Do you have someone checking into where the other inmate might go?" Wade asked. The two escapees were probably staying together. Cowards tended to do that. "Maybe it has nothing to do with the pamphlet Jasmine sent at all."

"That's possible. We're just covering all the bases."

Wade felt an elastic band inside him relax. He hadn't realized how tense he'd been. He knew he was pushing it, but he couldn't stop himself from asking. "So you don't really think Jasmine—Ms. Hunter—has much to do with it?"

"She might still be a destination. We plan to get some deputy sheriffs to keep an eye on the roads around here. But it doesn't take much to see that anyone coming into Dry Creek from outside wouldn't know how to find Ms. Hunter anyway. There aren't even any signs on most of these county roads."

"So you don't think she helped Lonnie escape?" Wade had to be sure.

"Not unless that's in code," the agent said with a laugh as he pointed to the copy of the pamphlet Wade held in his hand. "And so far we haven't seen any streets of gold or crosses on hillsides."

It hit Wade like a brick. There was a cross on a hill. It didn't belong to Jasmine, but—

"Are you okay?" the agent closest to him asked.

Wade brought his attention back. "Just a little hungry is all."

"Well, we're done here. We'll let you get to breakfast. The sheriff will be in touch with you about the deputies that are coming in."

"Good," Wade murmured as he watched the agents each put a ten dollar bill on the table and then stand up to leave.

"We'll see you later, Sutton. Let us know when your leg's better."

Wade nodded. That was about all that he could manage. As the agents left the café, he looked over at Jasmine. Had he lost the ability to see when something was suspicious? He was really slipping and this couldn't even be blamed on his leg.

Wade knew it was past nine o'clock. It was morning, but the sky outside was still gray and the sunlight was muted. Overhead lights had been turned on in the café. Without them, no one could read the menu. He looked around the large room. An old guitar hung on one wall with a plaque of some kind under it. A few snapshots of people were tacked up beside it. The linoleum in the floor was starting to wear in some places and the white curtains did not all match.

This whole town was full of ordinary people and ordinary places. He supposed it was the perfect hiding place for a clever criminal who was willing to put forth a little effort to blend into the scenery around here.

He knew he should stand up and walk back to the other table where Jasmine was sitting, but he was weary to the bone. He had disappointments he couldn't name because he'd never let himself believe his dreams could come true. The truth was he'd started to trust Jasmine. Care about her even. There was no fool like a lawman who should know better.

Someone turned a radio on in the kitchen and the music drifted out to him. He'd have to talk with Elmer later this morning and find out why he'd decided to erect that huge cross on the hill behind his barn. He'd need to know the sequence of events before he went to the agents with his suspicions.

He started to stand up and felt his leg cramp. The table was there so he held on to it for support. Maybe the doctors were right and it was time to think of a new career. And it wouldn't be because of his injury. He'd always said he'd be a lawman until he died, but he'd lost his taste for it. He had no appetite for putting Jasmine back in prison. Or anyone else, for that matter.

He looked up and saw Jasmine walking over to him.

"You okay?" she asked.

"Just my leg."

"Well, we can sit here," she said as she started to stack up the dirty dishes on the table. "I'll just take these back to Linda. She's on a long-distance phone call with her husband. Said she had more pancake batter ready to go if you'd like, though. And eggs with bacon."

"That sounds good," Wade said as he sank back down to the chair he'd been sitting in.

"Do you take your eggs fried or scrambled?" Jasmine asked.

"Fried."

Jasmine nodded and walked away with the dirty dishes. That's what was so confusing, he thought as he watched her go. The bad guys should act bad and the good guys good. It wasn't fair when everything got mixed up and someone who might be guilty tugged at a lawman's heart. Why was she being so nice?

As it turned out, Wade didn't have to wait to finish breakfast before he could talk to Elmer. The older man came over at the same time that Jasmine brought their full breakfast platters to the table. She claimed they had enough to share and went back to ask for another plate for her father.

"I heard the Feds were here," Elmer said when Jasmine walked back to the kitchen.

Just then the waitress came out of the kitchen and the two women started to laugh and talk as they went back through the door to the kitchen together. They were friends, Wade realized with a jolt. There would probably be a lot of people around here who would feel betrayed if his suspicions were true.

Wade nodded to Elmer. "The Feds have to check everything out."

"They're not giving any grief to Jasmine, though, are they?" the old man asked. "I have money, you know, if she needs a lawyer or anything."

"I know you do," Wade said, and he had no doubt the other man would mortgage his farm if he needed to on Jasmine's behalf. That's why it was so important Wade know the truth about some things.

"I've been wondering," he said. "That cross you have on the hill. What made you think of doing that?"

"I'm a grateful man," Elmer said.

"Well, you've been grateful other times in your life. Why did you put the cross up now?"

Elmer thought a minute. "I read an article in the paper about a man who put a statue of Jesus on his farm out by Great Falls. It kind of struck my fancy. A man should leave his mark on this world."

"Do you still have the newspaper article?"

"Well, now, I don't know. I think I gave it back to Jasmine. She was the one that handed it to me."

Wade would have to track down the article, but he felt relieved. It didn't sound like Jasmine had much to do with that cross. "Which newspaper was it?"

"It wasn't one I recognized. Must have been one of those throwaway ones."

Wade's heart sank. Anyone could print up a newspaper and pass it off as a throwaway.

Just then the kitchen door opened and Jasmine came walking out with a dinner plate and some silverware in her hand. "We're all set."

Wade let her sit down and begin dividing the pancakes and eggs before he asked her. "What kind of newspapers can I get around here anyway?"

"Billings is the closest," she said as she slid an egg onto a plate for Elmer. "Unless you want *USA TODAY* or something."

"Your father told me there was some small newspaper—that's where he got the idea to put up his cross."

Jasmine smiled at her father. "That's right."

"You don't happen to know what that paper was, do you? I'd like to read the article."

He watched her carefully to see if there was any trace of panic.

Jasmine just smiled at him. "Conrad gets it at his shop. I'll check the next time I'm at work. I don't know if he still has that issue or not. His place is closed next week because it's Christmas, but after that I should be able to get it for you—if he still has it—" Her voice trailed off. "If you're still here."

Wade nodded. He'd probably have to call Conrad himself and verify that Jasmine wasn't making everything up. He was getting a headache.

"You should stay, you know," Jasmine said suddenly.

"What?" Elmer asked as he looked at her.

Wade was just as surprised, but he was speechless and managed to keep his mouth shut.

She turned to her father. "Since Wade can't work with his leg being the way it is, he should stay. Spend some time with his grandfather. Go bowling with Carl. He'd like that—"

"Carl *bowls?* Where?" Wade asked.

Jasmine turned to him. "He and Barbara are trying to get a league formed in Miles City. Life is short. When was the last time you did something besides work?"

"I do lots of things besides work," Wade defended himself. He couldn't think straight. Was Jasmine saying she wanted him to stay in Dry Creek for a while? Well, of course, that's what she was saying. But why? "I ran in a marathon a couple of years ago. Took second place, too."

"Well, that's good," she said quietly.

He half expected her to ask him to stay again, but she didn't.

"People die in those marathons," Elmer said instead.

"They do not," Jasmine said, but Wade noticed her father didn't look relieved at that reassurance. It was clear the old man didn't trust him.

"I might be able to stay for a while," Wade said just to see Elmer's reaction. "And I'm here past Christmas anyway. With the pageant and all."

Jasmine groaned. "I forgot about the pageant."

"You don't need to do it," Elmer said firmly. "They still have that recording they can use. That works fine for the angel."

"But I want to do it," Jasmine said. "I just need to practice."

The thought of watching Jasmine play the role of the angel made the day seem brighter. "I'll be there to help. You'll want to be sure your halo is securely attached or it'll fall off."

"Don't tell me," Jasmine half asked.

"Yup, it happened to me. Landed right on the donkey's head." Wade nodded. "Kind of surprised the wise men. Made one of them drop their golden beads. They rolled around on the stage. Finally, the innkeeper had to come out with his broom and sweep them up so nobody would fall."

"I remember that," Elmer said with a grin. "The donkey kept shaking its head trying to get rid of the thing. And, of course, he wouldn't budge. Finally, he turned around and dumped the wise men in with the shepherds."

"Which made the shepherds cry," Wade added.

"That's because they used the kindergarten kids that year for shepherds," Elmer said. "My wife told them they were too young for the responsibility."

Wade nodded. "It isn't as easy to put on a pageant as everyone says."

Jasmine just laughed. "No one says that around here. Trust me."

Wade wished it *was* that easy to trust her. He looked at her face, all lit up with laughter, and he couldn't believe she'd ever done anything wrong in her life. But even believing she might be innocent was not the same as trusting. If he trusted her, he wouldn't need to have all of his questions answered. He'd know in the center of himself that she spoke the truth when she said she had nothing to do with Lonnie's escape. He wouldn't need proof.

He shook his head wistfully. How did a man begin to trust when he didn't naturally do it? And, it wasn't just Jasmine; he didn't trust anyone. That's the big reason why he never worked with a partner. He couldn't get used to having his life in someone else's hands.

Edith used to say that was his problem with

God—that he needed to let go and trust God to hold him or he'd never be able to trust anyone else, either. And she'd probably been right.

Usually, that was okay, though. It was just being back in Dry Creek that had him unnerved. It was a place so full of roots that people trusted each other in a way no one did in his apartment building in Idaho Falls. He couldn't even leave his rubber boots outside his door there, fearing some nameless neighbor would steal them. That life might be empty, but, if he had any sense, he'd pack up right now and go back. He didn't need to believe anything new to live there.

But, looking at Jasmine's face, he knew he wouldn't go. He couldn't bear to leave Dry Creek before Christmas. He wanted to see the look on her face as she soared overhead as an angel in that pageant. He had a feeling it was going to be something he'd remember as long as he lived.

Besides, if she was innocent, he didn't trust anyone else to keep her safe. And, if she was guilty, she'd still need him around to convince her to turn herself in. For the second time today, he wished he knew how to pray like he'd done as a boy before he'd lost all trace of faith. If he knew how, he'd close his eyes and pray for Jasmine.

Chapter Ten

Jasmine stood in the small hallway of her father's house. She was checking her lipstick in the mirror and generally avoiding the two men in the kitchen. She had accepted a dinner invitation from Conrad, thus causing herself more grief than if she had announced she was going on a date with an ax murderer from Mars.

"Didn't you say he'd be here by now?" her father called to her. He'd asked the same question three times already.

Wade and her father were sitting in the kitchen and drumming their fingers on the table. They'd been there for the past half hour and she had no desire to join them. They hadn't even turned a light on and it was growing dark outside.

"He said five-thirty," she called back. Conrad

had suggested they eat early when he'd seen the scowl Wade had given him in the café this morning. Conrad had come in the door as the lawman went back to the kitchen to pay Linda for their breakfast. By the time Wade came back and saw someone else was seated at their table, Conrad had already asked his question.

Jasmine wouldn't have said yes if she hadn't seen Wade's forbidding look. Just because he thought she was involved in Lonnie's escape, she didn't need to stay locked in her room. She's overheard enough of the conversation he'd had with the agents earlier to know that they didn't think she was in much danger. As they said, no one would even know how to find her unless someone in town told them.

"I think he's coming," her father called out. "Someone's pulling in."

Jasmine took one last look at herself. She'd finally gotten her hair to curl just right. She'd washed it this afternoon and the auburn color was subdued. She was wearing the gray wool skirt Edith liked so well. Her only jewelry was a leather watch so nothing she wore flashed or sparkled. She looked more like a librarian than an ex-con.

Of course, her black leather jacket didn't match the rest of her now, but she made do with what she had. Maybe she could convince her father to give her a sensible coat instead of that necklace for Christmas. Then she would blend right in around here. She might have wavered this morning, but she was determined to look like everyone else in this quiet town. By then she would be at ease with her new life.

Jasmine swung her purse over her shoulder and walked back to the kitchen.

"I don't know what the problem is. I'm not even leaving Dry Creek," she said as she continued over to the refrigerator and opened the freezer. "There are plenty of frozen dinners. Spaghetti. Tuna noodle. Pot roast. You can both help yourself."

"I'll wait until we get to the café," Wade said calmly from where he sat. He was wearing a denim shirt and jeans.

Jasmine gave him a severe look. "You can't follow me. I'm going on a date."

"He has to go with you," her father said with a nod to Wade. "He's only doing his job—keeping you safe."

Jasmine frowned. Sometime while they had been sitting at the table those two must have become allies. "Wade promised to bring you something back from the café, didn't he?"

"Just a hamburger," her father admitted. He

looked at Wade. "Grilled onions and pickles on the side. With maybe some fries."

"You got it," Wade said.

"I could bring you a hamburger, if that's what this is all about," Jasmine offered.

"Oh, I couldn't ask you to do that. You're going to be on a date."

"Exactly," she agreed. "And I don't need a chaperone."

"It's for your own good," her father protested. "Even if I don't get a hamburger, I'll feel better knowing there's someone with you to protect you just in case. I know Conrad's a nice young man, but I don't think he'd do too well in a fight."

"We're going out to eat, not to fight," she said as she heard a knock at the door. "That'll be him."

She walked to the door, but before she answered it, she turned back. "You two be nice now."

Neither one of the men answered her as she opened the door.

Conrad had an anxious look on his face. He stood lean and tall, his brown hair slicked back. He stood in the doorway a minute, running his fingers under the black tie he wore with his beige shirt. His black wool coat hung open in the front.

Jasmine was glad she'd dressed as conservatively as she had. She matched him that way.

Conrad didn't seem any more inclined to talk than her father and Wade were. He nodded at both men and then held the door for her as she left. There was some bite to the cold air and they both walked quickly to his car. He opened the passenger door for her and she slid into the warm interior.

"Nice music," she said as Conrad opened the driver's door and moved into place behind the wheel.

"I knew you'd like it," Conrad said.

Actually, the hymns on his CD were a little slow for her taste, but she figured she would appreciate them more if she listened to the words carefully. The slow rhythm was probably more holy than the stuff she liked anyway. She'd get used to it.

Conrad started his car and backed up before heading into Dry Creek.

"That's some cross you've got up there on the hill," Conrad said as he turned onto the main gravel road. "I could see it on the way out here—even from the edge of Dry Creek."

"It's my father's. Sort of a Christmas thing he's got going."

Conrad nodded. "My uncle put a lit-up snowman on his roof. It's got a mechanical arm that waves all night long. You'll have to take your father and drive by some time. Get the effect."

Jasmine noticed that Conrad kept looking in the rearview mirror, but she refused to turn around.

"Dry Creek should have a contest. Best outdoor decorations," she said, hoping to keep Conrad distracted. It didn't work.

"Is he *following* us?" Conrad finally asked as he turned his head to look behind them.

Jasmine knew it was pointless to pretend she didn't know who Conrad meant. "I think he's just going to get some hamburgers."

"Because if he's worried about that guy coming to town while you're with me, he doesn't need to. I can take care of an escaped fel—" Conrad stopped. He just realized what he'd said. "Well, I can take care of things. That's the point."

Jasmine nodded. She supposed it had been too much to expect that everyone wouldn't find out what was going on. "Who told you?"

Conrad looked over at her. "Charley heard it this morning from Elmer. But you can't blame them. I heard it from Linda later, too. She knew because the agents went back and asked her to be on the lookout for the guy. If he came to town, they figured he'd go to the café first to ask directions."

Jasmine felt a little ill. She hadn't thought of that. "I hope they didn't tell her to do anything. I don't want anyone to get hurt."

She would need to make it plain to Linda that she wasn't to let on that she knew who Lonnie was if he came by. She should just give him the directions he asked for. Better yet, Linda should close the café for the next week or so. She hadn't taken a vacation since she went to London this past summer with her guitar-playing husband.

But if the café was closed, Lonnie would just go to the hardware store. Maybe they should close for a few days, too. Which would leave the church. Or the houses themselves. The queasy feeling got worse. No one would be safe in Dry Creek if Lonnie was headed here.

"You okay?" Conrad asked. "I'm sorry if I wasn't supposed to know about that guy—"

"No. It's good that you know. Everyone should know. Everyone needs to leave Dry Creek."

"What?"

"Oh, just for a few days. Until the Feds catch Lonnie."

"We can't all just leave. Where would we go?"

Linda thought of that necklace her father was giving her for Christmas. She could sell it for a few thousand. "Those hot springs. You know, those mineral baths over by Dillion. They have some real deals this time of year."

"People can't afford—"

"I could pay," she said. Her teeth were starting to chatter. It was warm in the car, but she felt a chill inside that wouldn't go away. "We could all go together. It would be fun."

"The whole *town?*"

"Of course. People are always complaining about their aches and pains. It'd be perfect."

Conrad didn't have much else to say for the rest of the drive into town. Neither did Jasmine. She was too focused on trying to remember if she'd passed any pawn shops in Miles City when she'd been there. It would be a pity to pawn a necklace like the one she was getting for Christmas, but it was the quickest way to have money.

If she hadn't been so worried about what might happen, she would have thought more about where she and Conrad were going. She didn't really think about it until they pulled into Dry Creek and she noticed how dark the windows of the café were.

Saturday night was date night at the café and Linda always dimmed the lights and put candles on the tables. She pushed the larger tables to one side of the room, too, so that she could position the smaller tables in strategic places around the rest of the café. She managed to give the illusion of a dozen alcoves each with a private table for two. The Redferns were already sitting at one of the tables, holding hands as they gazed into each other's eyes. The rodeo guy, Zach Lucas, and his new wife were at another.

"Welcome," Linda said in a hushed voice as she walked over to Conrad and Jasmine as they entered the café. She was wearing a black skirt with a white blouse and carrying several large menu sheets. "Where would you care to sit?"

Jasmine wasn't worried about sitting anywhere, but she knew Linda was proud of her "romance corners," as she called them. She even had her radio in the back tuned to a station that played love songs. They had more rhythm than Conrad's hymns.

"Closest to the door is good," Jasmine said when Conrad looked over at her for her opinion.

"By the door, it is then," Linda said as she led them there.

They were barely seated before the door to the café opened and Wade walked inside.

Jasmine knew Linda needed to go seat her next guest, but she wanted to start her thinking about a small vacation. "Have you ever been to one of those hot springs west of here? Where the water bubbles up out of the ground?"

"The mineral baths? I've always thought they

look lovely. I think I have some brochures in the back. Don't tell me you're going to one of them?"

"Maybe," Jasmine said. She wondered why she hadn't sent Lonnie a brochure for some vacation place instead of that pamphlet on heaven. At least then no one would think he might come up here.

The truth was, though, that she had wanted Lonnie to get a glimpse of God. Her ex-partner wasn't supposed to break out of jail, but he was supposed to break free of some of the guilt he must feel for all he'd done in his life. She'd do as much for her worst enemy.

"Our special tonight is grilled salmon with lemon sauce," Linda said.

"Sounds good to me," Conrad said as he laid the menu down on the table and looked at Jasmine. "How about you?"

Jasmine nodded. She was barely listening. Thinking of Lonnie made her realize, she certainly didn't deserve to be sitting here with a nice man like Conrad. However, as bad as her past was, she'd feel a hundred times worse if something happened to anyone in Dry Creek because of Lonnie.

"You don't know of a place to sell jewelry, do you?" she asked Conrad.

"Me?" He shook his head. "I know a consignment shop that takes old ties, but that's about it."

She reached into her purse and pulled out the crumpled green notebook she'd borrowed from Wade this morning. Then she stood up. "I'll be right back."

Jasmine walked over to Wade. He was sitting at a table across the room. He had a jacket on and she wondered if he wore his gun in a holster under it.

"Don't they ever put the lights on in this place?" Wade grumbled before she even got all the way to his table. She noticed he'd blown his candle out. "It's dark in here."

"It's supposed to be romantic."

He grunted. "It's dangerous as all get-out."

"I forgot to give this back earlier," she said when she got to the table and could offer it to him.

He looked at the notebook in her hand and then up to her. "No problem."

"About my dad—"

He took the notebook and waved her words aside. "Don't worry about it. We've made our peace. I can't blame him for coming on strong. He'd do anything for you."

Jasmine smiled. "I know. That's why I need to find a place that buys old jewelry. I figure you would know one from your work. If you could write down the name and as much of the address as you know, I'd appreciate it."

Wade went very still. "What kind of jewelry are we talking here?"

"A diamond-and-ruby necklace that retails for ten to fifteen thousand, maybe more if there are earrings with it."

"And you want to cash it out?"

Jasmine nodded. "I'd prefer to pawn it so I could buy it back, but I have an idea and it'll require some capital."

She knew she should explain herself more fully. But she just leaned back and watched the war in Wade's eyes. He wasn't sure whether he needed to be suspicious or not. She turned around before she could see what he finally decided. She already knew that he didn't trust her.

"Just list the places," she said over her shoulder as she walked back to the table where Conrad was patiently waiting.

She spent the rest of the evening being annoyed with Wade while searching for things to talk to Conrad about. She knew Conrad was trying to come up with conversation, too. Finally, they both gave up and started to talk about the engines he had in his shop that needed repair. The shop was closed for a long Christmas break, but the two of them would be back after New Year's. They spoke low and kept their heads together so Linda couldn't hear them. The café owner would be appalled to hear anyone talking about engine repairs on date night.

Chapter Eleven

Wade was sitting on the porch at his grandfather's house, watching the sun start to rise. He had his sleeping bag wrapped around him and a thermos of hot coffee at his feet. The deputies wouldn't be in place until tomorrow and he wanted to be sure all was calm until then. No one had gone past his grandfather's house, heading over to the Maynard place, since Conrad had left last night.

Speaking of that man, he was too skinny to be of much use in a fight. And he had a startled, rabid look in his eyes when Wade studied him for too long. It shouldn't, but it made Wade feel good to know the other man was so easily unnerved. He told himself it meant Conrad was too timid for someone like Jasmine.

Of course, she didn't seem to know that. Wade's heart had sunk last night as he saw the two of them lean in and start talking together in hushed voices. Whatever it was they were talking about, it had them both captivated.

Jasmine had even forgotten to come back and get the notebook she'd left. He still had it in his pocket and he'd written an address down for her. Plus, he'd added the name of someone to talk to there just to show he couldn't care less who she ate dinner with.

Oh, who was he kidding?

The whole night had given him heartburn. And he hadn't rushed through his meal so that wasn't the problem. No, it was watching Jasmine and her date that bothered him. He didn't know why she couldn't sit and talk to him with that rapt look on her face.

Not that he should be jealous. He was guarding her, not courting her. Besides, she was halfway to being a suspect and only a fool got involved with one of those.

Wade supposed he'd just been single too long. There was a fine line between being a carefree bachelor and being a hopeless hermit and he might be skidding too close to the latter. Last night had brought that home to him. It seemed like every happily married couple in Dry Creek had come into the café to hold hands and coo over each other. They'd all nodded to him as they passed his table, but he still felt like a freak.

He wondered if it wasn't against the law for a public café to have a night that discriminated against single, dateless people like that. There was nothing worse than sitting alone and eating by candlelight in a room reeking with romance.

At least Linda had been gracious enough to make up a thermos of vegetable soup for his grand-father. And, she'd given him some dinner rolls and a few hard-boiled eggs, as well. The old man had been happy to have them when Wade came to the door last night. His grandfather still called him Sonny, but he seemed content to have him around. Wade told himself he'd have to get his grandfather to a doctor after Christmas. And, in the meantime, he might as well clean the place up some.

Not today, though, he thought as he looked at the sky. Today was Sunday and, after he went out to the barn and made sure Jenny was fed, he needed to pick Jasmine up and take her to the pageant practice. One good thing was that Conrad wouldn't be able to best him in giving advice to Jasmine. There was a brotherhood among those who had managed to fly as the angel that others just wouldn't understand. She didn't have to be innocent for him to help in her role as an angel. It was nice that they had something that didn't involve the law.

Jasmine was up and dressed when Wade came to the door. She was wearing a gray sweater over a white T-shirt and blue jeans. Her eyes looked tired and he wondered if she'd spent the night thinking about Conrad.

"Trouble in paradise?" he asked.

She hefted her purse onto her shoulder and turned to scoop up a garment bag from a nearby kitchen chair. "Nothing I can't handle."

"No doubt," he said.

She moved the garment bag and he could see it was slipping.

"Let me," he said as he stepped closer and held out a hand.

"Thanks," she said as she turned to look behind the door and came out with a four-foot tall cardboard cutout.

"Those are your wings?" Wade guessed, not entirely sure.

She nodded. "The kindergartners made them in Sunday school."

"Oh." He looked at them skeptically. "Aren't they a little bent?"

Streaks of silver glitter went the length of the wings and cotton balls were glued here and there on the cardboard. The right wing was the one that curled in at the tip. It looked like it'd fold in a breeze.

Jasmine smiled fondly at the wings. "That's because they're made out of the box that Linda's new refrigerator came in. There were corners and we had to straighten them. Little Bobbie sat on them but we didn't get them completely smooth."

Wade wasn't reassured. "Maybe if you'd added some wire reinforcement."

"I didn't want to risk anyone getting hurt. Besides, wire's too hard for the kindergarten kids to use."

"These wings could fall off," Wade felt duty-bound to point out. "Then what would you do?"

"Well, it's not like I need them to fly. Besides, I'm lucky I didn't end up with a dragon tail. The kids got into this, but some of them didn't know what angels looked like in the back. They'd seen angel pictures from the front, of course, but that didn't satisfy them as to the unseen part of an angel. One boy thought they should be more like dragons in the back."

Wade couldn't imagine an angel with a more delightful back than the one standing right here holding these wings. "At least the shepherds would be awestruck if they saw a dragon, though."

"I don't think I was ever supposed to breathe fire or anything. I think the wings just seemed a little tame to them. They see so many things on television."

"What kind of a world do we live in when seeing a creature with wings doesn't strike fear in a little boy's heart?"

"A world with computer games and movies," she said as she followed him out the door. "Kids haven't been easy to impress since *Star Wars.*"

As they walked to his car, Wade looked down at what he was carrying. "Hey, this is the same bag they used for the angel costume when I was a kid."

Jasmine grinned. "Same bag. Same costume."

"Really?" He remembered what seemed like a zip-up bathrobe made out of white satin. The folds of fabric had gotten in the way of his legs and the whole thing felt slippery. Which was part of the reason he hadn't been able to get that bag of dimes opened like he'd planned.

"They did get a few new costumes donated this year," Jasmine said. "But so far no white angel ones."

"By donated, you don't mean bathrobes?" he said as he opened the trunk.

Jasmine nodded as she put her wings inside. "I understand it's a tradition that all of the costumes are recycled bathrobes coming from local people who don't need them any longer."

Wade grunted. "I would have thought they'd have sprung for some regular costumes during all these years. Bathrobes don't improve with age."

He laid the garment bag with the costume over the wings and shut the trunk.

"Well, they do try to match the bathrobe to the role," Jasmine said as they walked to the passenger door and Wade opened it. "I understand some people even buy their bathrobes thinking they'd make a good costume for this or that part. Of course, it takes years to wear out a bathrobe. And who wants to look like a shepherd?"

Jasmine slid into the passenger seat and reached for her seat belt. Wade closed her door and walked around to open his own.

"If they were going to take up a collection around here, they should have taken it to buy some decent costumes instead of worrying about me," Wade muttered as he took his place behind the wheel.

Jasmine grinned over at him. "Oh, the bathrobes are part of the fun. Besides, it keeps the community active in the pageant."

"I can't believe anyone needs to worry about people getting behind the pageant. Folks used to come over from Miles City," Wade paused as he started his car. "Even some from Billings, I think."

"People don't come to Dry Creek as much as they used to. Not that we've given up trying to get them here. That's part of the reason the pastor's wife and her niece painted that huge mural on the side of the barn. It has some historic significance. Everybody wants to see something special."

"I would think the nativity would be special enough," Wade said before he realized he sounded just like Edith. He sure wasn't one to point fingers at people who didn't go to a Christmas pageant. He hadn't been inside a church for decades and he usually spent Christmas Eve in front of his television.

He turned onto the main road before he realized something. "I didn't see Elmer. Is he coming to practice, too?"

"I think he's avoiding it," Jasmine said. "He went over to visit Charley."

Wade had talked to Charley briefly last night when the other man had brought Edith to the café for a cup of tea. Charley had said then that he wasn't going to this morning's practice, either, so he'd given directions to Wade regarding the angel wheel. The morning was looking better now that it was just him and Jasmine driving down the road.

The skies were clear and there didn't seem much chance of snow.

He knew he'd be sorry that he was letting his guard down around Jasmine, but he did want to spend some time talking to her. No matter how this all turned out, he wanted her to know he wished her well.

"Would you mind stopping at the café first?" Jasmine asked after a few minutes.

"It's not open on Sunday, is it?"

"I just want to post a notice next to the door. You know on that bulletin board where they have the menu."

"I hope you're not planning a yard sale or anything." He sounded like a grumpy old man, but he couldn't call the words back so he continued. "Usually you need a permit for something like that."

"Not in Dry Creek." Jasmine's lips pressed tight together. "This is a town of harmony and peace. We don't bother with the small stuff like permits."

Wade knew he should just nod and agree, but he didn't. "Every town has some problems."

"Not this one," Jasmine snapped back and then blinked a few times. "Well, except for me, of course."

Wade almost pulled off the road and stopped the car, but he was only a few hundred yards from the café so he waited to pull in there before he parked and turned to Jasmine. "What in the world are you talking about? No one here thinks you're a problem. In fact, it's the opposite. Everyone goes around singing your praises."

"That's only because they don't know," Jasmine said, and a tear slid down her cheek.

There was probably some regulation some-where that told a lawman what he was supposed to do in this case, but Wade had never heard of it. He slid a little farther over on the seat so he could put his arm around Jasmine's shoulder. "It can't be that bad. Whatever it is, we can fix it."

He could feel a silent hiccup shake Jasmine's shoulders.

"I need to post my notice," she said.

"I'll post it for you. You just sit here and hold your breath. That should make the hiccups go away," Wade said.

Jasmine bent down and rummaged in her purse before she came up with a sheet of paper that she held out to him.

Wade didn't even stop to read it. He just grabbed it and opened his car door.

He was at the bulletin board, searching for another thumbtack, before he actually looked at the paper. "What in the world?"

Jasmine had drawn a map of the Dry Creek area and put a red star where she lived with her father. Then she put in bold block letters: Find Jasmine Here.

He forgot all about the thumbtack and went back to his car. He slid into the driver's seat before turning to her.

"What's this?" he demanded as he shook the paper in his hand. "Are you telling Lonnie how to find you?"

She nodded her head.

Wade's heart sank.

"I have to," she said in a small voice. "If I don't tell him, people could be hurt."

Now she was crying in earnest.

He put his arm out and this time she slid into his embrace.

"Now start from the beginning," Wade said. His voice was gentle and he hadn't even had to think about it. "Tell me what you mean."

It took a couple of minutes, because of a few tears and some lingering hiccups, but Jasmine told him what she'd concluded about Lonnie coming to town and trying to find out where she lived from people.

"He's got a bad temper," she said in conclusion. "I can't have him going around here hurting people if they don't tell him what he wants to know."

Wade smoothed back her hair. "So you figured you'd just tell him what he wanted so he wouldn't need to ask?"

She nodded. "At first I thought about taking everyone to the hot springs over by Dillion. But with Christmas being so close, that wouldn't work. People want to be home. With kids and everything, you know—"

Wade smiled. So that's what she'd been talking about last night. He'd thought she and Conrad had those hot springs planned for the two of them. Which just went to show that a man could be wrong.

"We can post a note if you feel better, but we'll make a fake one. Lead him down a false path. Or maybe just a confusing one."

"I wouldn't want him to go to somebody else's house," Jasmine said.

"We won't send him anywhere but around in circles. If he takes the map off the board, though, Linda might see and be able to call the sheriff's department. That way they'd know where he was headed. There are enough county roads out here to keep him lost for days."

Jasmine nodded slowly. "I guess that would work."

"We'll make a new notice after practice this morning," Wade agreed as he handed the map back to Jasmine. "Save that for something more important."

"I just—" Jasmine looked up at him, her eyes still moist. "The people here don't understand what they have. I know because I've never had it in my life before. This is a special place for me."

Wade nodded. "I know what you mean."

"No one should be hurt here."

Wade knew he was going to kiss her when she said that. He couldn't help himself. He'd made protecting people his life's work, but he never cared about those people, not up close and personal. Not like Jasmine.

He smoothed a tear away and then, with her cuddled close in his arms, he bent his lips to kiss her. He felt the sentiment rush up inside him and he knew he was hooked.

Chapter Twelve

A thin stream of early morning light filtered into the barn and the air was dusty. Weathered boards rose high on each side of the huge structure and the view, as Jasmine made her swing, went from the rafters straight down to the wooden plank floor below. No one was down there, which was a good thing because her fingers were cold as they gripped the ropes that held her aloft. She wouldn't be able to give an angel wave to anyone. And, of course, her hair was a whirlwind of a mess.

But she had her wings strapped to her back and she was soaring.

Better yet, she was happy inside. Not just because she was going to be an angel in the world's best pageant. No, she was all warm and fuzzy inside because Wade had kissed her and he hadn't made any apology afterward or suggested she fill out a complaint form or anything. Instead, he'd given a big whoop and grinned at her until she had to grin back.

She looked toward the hayloft just so she could gaze at him again. He was staring down at the gears, making sure the wheel worked and her flight was smooth, but she could still see a slight smile on his face. Yes, it was a happy day.

She felt the rush of air as she flew back over the barn. She was glad she didn't have to worry about her costume because she was still in jeans. She'd only been up in the angel swing one other time with Charley at the wheel, but last night the older man had stopped to tell her Wade would run the contraption as there was some vet work Charley needed to do this morning. He'd promised to be at the real performance tonight.

Wade had read the directions and made a test flight himself before he let her get in the rope harness. At first, he'd thought she should wait for everyone to come, but she explained how quickly the kids would get accustomed to her flying and how she wanted them to look up at her with as much awe as possible on Christmas Eve.

She swung back to where she'd started and Wade was there to catch her. Her body landed against his with a soft thud. He'd braced his feet to catch her and small bits of loose hay, separated from the stacked bales, flew up in the air. Wade didn't seem to mind, though, and he held her for a minute, angel wings and all, purring in her ear and making her heart race. She looked up at him with a smile. His eyes were warm and he traced her cheek with his thumb.

Jasmine was sure he was going to kiss her again.

But then the door to the barn below opened with a bang and a couple of dozen kids came running inside. Edith followed them and Jasmine knew the older woman would need help so she asked Wade to unhook her so she could go down.

"You could help, too," she suggested as he undid her from the rigging and then helped her take off the wings.

"I don't know much about kids."

"So learn. You were a kid once. It's like that bicycle thing—it'll come back to you." Jasmine leaned the wings against a stack of hay bales. She'd leave them there until tonight.

Wade grunted, but he looked pleased that she was inviting him to help. They both climbed down the ladder to the main part of the barn.

"Oh, there you are," Edith said when she saw them. "I think we need to break up into small groups and practice the various parts individually before we put them all together for the pageant. Wade, can you take the boys over there? Girls, I'll be with you along the other wall. Just give me a second."

Jasmine was not surprised when Edith turned to her when the kids, along with Wade, started to move into groups.

"You have to tell me all about it," Edith whispered with joy in her voice. "I couldn't wait to hear. It's time you were dating."

"How did you see through everything?" Jasmine whispered back, with a tilt in her voice. She knew Edith had said Wade wasn't ready to trust anyone and she knew he didn't go to church so she'd have to pray for him about that, but eventually, maybe—

"Conrad was so excited," Edith continued, her voice bubbling even though she spoke low. "He said he had such a good time and, of course, you both have so much in common and—"

Jasmine's heart sank. Conrad. Of course.

"He's a good man," Jasmine forced herself to say. She suddenly felt very tired. "The kind of man any woman would be proud to call her friend."

"And he respects you, too," Edith gushed. "That's important."

Jasmine nodded. Conrad was exactly the kind

of a man she should pick to gradually get to know and then peacefully marry. He was steady, faithful and safe. He didn't use a gun to make his living and he went to church. He was perfect.

She looked across the barn at Wade. There was nothing gradual or peaceful or perfect about him. Even if he did come back to the church, he'd argue with God. He wasn't the kind of man who could let things go. If he was upset, he would show it.

She lifted her arm to smooth down her hair.

Edith reached into the purse she was carrying and pulled out a CD. "Conrad said to give this to you. He said you'd liked it last night and he meant to give it to you before you left, but—" The older woman raised an eyebrow. "He apparently got distracted."

Jasmine forced herself to smile as she took the CD. "Thanks."

She wondered if she should tell Edith that Conrad had gotten distracted because they were talking about the new combines that were supposed to come to the county fair this summer.

"Charley and I want to have the two of you over for dinner sometime soon," Edith continued, her face pink with excitement. "It won't be quite as romantic as date night at the café, but we'd love to have you."

Jasmine nodded.

"We have a very romantic swing on the porch. I love to sit out there with Charley in the evenings. We look up at the stars."

"Wonderful."

"Well, I better go see to the girls," Edith said as she turned to look toward one wall and then the other. "Wade seems to be doing fine with the boys."

Jasmine followed Edith's gaze. Yes, Wade did seem to be doing well.

Wade knew he was in trouble. He'd worked a couple of hostage negotiations in his day and he was used to staring down the business end of a gun. Nothing had prepared him for boys in a tangle, though.

"It's not *our* fault they were promised a donkey," a shepherd with the fresh bruise on his cheek said as he pointed his finger at the three wise men. "If we have to walk, they have to walk. The wise men just think they're better than us because they've got that gold and stuff. Everybody knows it's only plastic. You can't even buy anything with it. "

Wade nodded because the boy seemed to expect it.

"But we're coming from *afar*," the tallest of the

three wise men whined in protest. His voice was a little nasal. "You shepherds are just up there in the hills like you always are. No one will believe we are from *afar* if we walk up like we were just next door buying something at the store."

"Maybe you came by bus," a different shepherd boy replied. "Then you'd be walking from the bus stop."

The wise man snorted in disbelief. "They didn't have buses back then. Or bus stops, either. I don't think they even had rubber tires for buses. Or gasoline. Or windshields. Or—"

Wade tuned the rest of the list out. The crux of the problem, as far as he could determine, was that Edith still hadn't located a donkey and the wise men thought some of the shepherds should abandon their flocks and pull a chariot for them as they made their entrance. He wondered if the Romans had chariots at the time Jesus was born. He supposed they did.

Finally, the list ended and Wade leaned over so he could get a better handle on the negotiations. He was bending from the waist and keeping his leg straight, but his muscles were still protesting so he changed position slightly until he found some relief.

"I'm not going to be no donkey," the first

shepherd boy declared with his hands curled into fists.

The wise man that had made the list looked at Wade a little smugly. "Tell them they have to be a donkey if that's the part they're assigned. We all need to do the parts we are assigned. Even if it's being a donn-n—key." The boy drew the word out and got a laugh, at least from the other wise men.

The shepherds didn't think it was so funny.

Wade was tempted to call Edith in to mediate, but he figured he wasn't done yet.

Just then the youngest of the shepherds slid in close and whispered in Wade's ear, "They're teasing me because I have to wear a pink bathrobe."

Wade looked at all the boys.

"First off, it's not a bathrobe. It's a costume," he told everyone before looking down at the boy with the complaint. "And pink is just a washed-out red. Fire trucks are red. That's a man's color. You'll do fine."

The boy didn't look convinced, but he took his thumb out of his mouth.

"Secondly, we *need* the shepherds," he said to the other boys. "Don't think you're not important. If it weren't for you, no one would have been there to gather around the baby Jesus on that night."

"Well, the wise men—"

Wade gave the three of them a stern look. "And, thirdly, if the kindergarten kids could make angel wings out of a cardboard delivery box, you can make a donkey out of something. You've got to be, what, nine or ten years old? You wise men need to figure out how to make what you need and the rest of us will help."

Wade was proud of himself until he noticed that all of the boys were looking at him as though he had disappointed them. "What?"

"I thought you were supposed to be a sheriff," the first shepherd said in disgust. "You should lock those wise men up for bothering us. Disturbing our peace."

"Us? You're the ones who—" the wise man started in.

Wade put two fingers in his mouth and gave a shrill whistle. Everything stopped.

"I need to sit down," he said. "And when I do, I want you to be in two separate groups. Wise men to my left. Shepherds to my right."

He went to the side of the barn and brought back a folding chair. Then he sat down.

"Left." He pointed since no one except him had moved and then he reversed directions. "Right."

"Are we going to fight?" the bathrobe shepherd asked with enthusiasm.

"No, we're going to do crafts."

Wade remembered, when there were problems with him many years ago, Edith always turned to crafts. She used to say that busy hands were happy hands.

"What do you know about crafts?" the wise man scoffed.

"More than you'd expect, son. More than you'd expect."

The wise men finally went into a huddle a few feet away to talk about how to make a donkey, so Wade only had the shepherds to deal with.

"You could make sheep," Wade suggested as they sat there looking bored.

The boys shook their heads in unison. "We got sheep. Our dogs. We already got the white towels to put on them and everything."

The boys sat there, cross-legged, and in a circle around his chair.

"Being a shepherd is dumb anyway," one boy finally complained.

Wade expected the others to contradict him, but they didn't. They all just sat in the circle looking as if they'd been left out of the fun of the pageant.

"Even the innkeeper gets to talk," the boy continued his grievance. "We don't have nothing to say."

"Well, shepherds are still important," Wade said after a minute. "They have to feed the sheep—"

A couple of the boys grunted, but it wasn't a sign of any enthusiasm.

"—and they have to protect the sheep," he continued.

"Do they have guns?" the bathrobe boy asked. He perked up at that thought. "You can't protect nothing without a gun."

"You should know that, being a sheriff," another shepherd added with some persuasion in his voice.

"A gun is always a last resort," Wade said to the boys.

"I bet a real shepherd would have a gun," the oldest boy challenged him.

"Nobody had a gun in the Bible." Wade was beginning to enjoy himself with these boys. It wouldn't hurt them to ask a question or two. He could handle it.

"That's because they just prayed instead," the bathrobe boy said with a sigh. "That's what my mom always says I should do is pray about it, pray about it, pray about it."

"Well, ah—" Wade cleared his throat. "You should always do what your mother says."

"You mean, we should pray about the wise

men?" the boy asked, looking up at Wade with trust in his eyes.

"I don't— I, ah—" Wade stammered. He was no authority on prayer. He hadn't said a prayer since he'd been a boy and pleaded with God to either bring back his mother or his father. He had been so desperate for a family, he'd have settled for Him finding a distant aunt or uncle. God's refusal to answer had shown him one thing. God didn't listen to Wade Sutton so there was no point in talking to Him. How could he explain something like that to these boys, though? They might be bloodthirsty, but they trusted God.

"I haven't prayed for a long time," he finally said softly.

"That's okay," the oldest of the shepherds said as he put his hand out to Wade. "We'll show you how."

Wade didn't know whether to laugh or cry. The boys swept him up into their circle of prayer and tried to share their faith with him. They blessed each of their dogs and told God how they felt the wise men were being unfair and that they needed a donkey. They confessed, they requested, they believed. Wade could see plainly the bottom line was that they believed God was going to come through for them.

He didn't want them to stop praying, but he

was nervous by the time they'd finished. Wade hoped they never lost their way like he had, but God wasn't likely to answer their prayers, either. Oh, He might bless their dogs now, but the animals would eventually die. And the wise men were still going to be there tomorrow to lord it over them. Some bathrobes would always be pink and not everyone got to talk. Life didn't always deliver up what people prayed for.

But the donkey! Wade suddenly realized he might be able to do something about the donkey.

"Nobody move," Wade commanded as he stood. "I'll be right back."

He walked over to where Jasmine and Edith were talking to the girls. They were part of some choir that sang in the background during the manger scene. They must be planning a song or two for the time before all the cast sang "Silent Night." He caught Edith's eye and motioned her over to the edge of the circle.

Jasmine had her back to him, but he could hear her voice as she softly sang along with the girls. She had one arm around a little girl and looked as natural as if she was a mother herself. For the first time, he realized what Jasmine had given up during all those years in prison. She should have a home and family of her own. She should be stealing kisses with a husband instead of a stray lawman like him. An unexpected wistfulness stabbed through him.

Then he looked up and saw Edith watching him thoughtfully.

"Do you still need a donkey?" he asked before she could comment. He cleared his throat and frowned.

She nodded. "I was going to stop by and ask your grandfather, but—"

"I'll do it," he said as he turned slightly so he didn't need to meet her eyes. "I saw an old horse trailer beside the barn this morning when I was checking on Jenny. I'll bring her over tomorrow night in plenty of time for the pageant. My grandfather won't mind."

"Why that'd be wonderful," Edith said and he made the mistake of looking back at her. She beamed at him cautiously for a second, but then the wattage gradually increased until her whole face was literally glowing.

"And there's an old bathrobe of mine in the closet at my grandfather's house," he continued as he tried to make his face look blank. No one needed to see his heart hanging out there like it had been. "Maybe we could switch out the pink one."

Edith nodded. "The boys will be thrilled." She paused and turned her head slightly as if she wanted to say something, but all she got out was, "What a great day this is."

"Oh," he added. "If any of the boys ask, Jesus didn't carry a gun."

"What?" Edith blinked.

Wade grinned. That would give his friend something to think about instead of the lovestruck look she'd seen on his face while he'd stared at Jasmine.

The door opened before he got back to the shepherds and Carl walked into the barn. Wade motioned for him to come over and join him and the boys. He knew the sheriff was there to update him, but Carl might have a minute after that to tell the boys that guns never solved anything.

"You want me to say *what?*" Carl asked when they met up in the middle of the barn. The boys were still sitting over where Wade had left them. They couldn't hear, but he lowered his voice anyway.

"Just encourage them to solve their problems *without* guns or their fists. Or arguing—put that one in there, too. Arguing can be bad."

"What am I supposed to tell them to do about these problems then?" Carl looked bewildered.

"Tell them to obey their mothers and pray."

Carl looked at him. "Remember, we're the law around here. Sometimes we need to raise our voices—and do more than pray that things will change."

"I know." Wade sighed. "I just don't want them to turn out like—"

He stopped.

"Like us?" Carl asked.

Wade shook his head. "No, just not like me. You're doing okay."

"Well," Carl started, as if he was going so say something encouraging, but then he looked Wade straight in the eyes. "If you don't like what you've become, then maybe it's time you changed."

Wade was a little startled at his friend's frankness. "I don't—"

Carl waved his words aside. "You've had this chip on your shoulder since we were boys. When you left church all those years ago, you changed. So, God didn't do exactly what you wanted."

"All I wanted was a family."

Carl nodded. "And God gave you a family."

"My grandfather wasn't exactly—"

"I meant the church here. After you ran off with your father, folks spent hours trying to find you, especially after your dad was killed. They put ads in newspapers. They took turns driving to all the little towns in the state where they thought you might have gone. They searched for well over a year. Finally, they figured you didn't want to be found."

Wade was silent. He'd gone over to Seattle and gotten a job as a dishwasher. He'd had no idea anyone in Dry Creek would even miss him.

"It was always easier for you to hide than to let yourself be found," Carl finally said wearily. "I'm not casting any stones. I was the same way for a lot of years."

"But you changed."

The sheriff nodded. "Yes, I changed. That's why I know you can, too."

With that, the two men started walking over to meet with the boys. Wade felt like he was shaken to his core. Had he really missed God's answer to all his boyhood prayers? Was he so busy being angry that he didn't even know what he could have?

He looked over at where Jasmine stood and asked the hardest question of all. Was he going to miss it all again? Was it even possible for a man who'd lived his life alone to trust someone else? If he prayed now, would God even listen?

Wade shook his head; he just didn't know the answer to any of his questions. And he couldn't just listen to his heart anyway, not until he knew about Jasmine and Lonnie.

Chapter Thirteen

Jasmine had seen the sheriff come into the barn and she waited for him to finish talking to Wade before she excused herself from the choir and walked over to the men. If they had something they wanted to say to her, she didn't want them to say it around the children. The little ones didn't need to be reminded that their Christmas angel was an ex-con and still under suspicion of doing something wrong.

Carl met her eyes when she got close.

"Hey, I got those fireworks you wanted," the sheriff said. "I have them out in the car. Got them from a guy in Miles City."

"Did he have sparklers? That's really what I wanted." Jasmine glanced at Wade and saw him smile as he listened.

"You'll have to look in the bag," Carl said with a shrug. "He just gave me what he had."

"I'll help you look," Wade offered as he started to turn.

"Before anyone moves, I have good news," the sheriff said. "I think we're in the clear. The Feds don't think Lonnie is planning to come up this way. They've talked to some of the other prisoners and they believe the other escapee was the brains behind the break. They think the two of them will head down to Mexico. That's the smart thing for them to do."

"Well, that's a relief," Jasmine said. She felt muscles inside her relax that she hadn't even known were tensed.

"It's just—" the sheriff said, and then hesitated. He looked over at Wade. "It's probably nothing."

"A hunch?" Wade asked.

The sheriff nodded and then looked over at Jasmine. "The other thing the inmates said is that Lonnie always used to talk about you. In kind of weird ways. How you were his soul mate and how the two of you were meant to be together and stuff like that."

"He's nuts," Jasmine said. The thought of Lonnie talking about her being with her made her skin crawl.

"Probably," the sheriff said. "Just to be on the safe side, we'll have deputy sheriffs posted around town for a few days. They'll take turns sitting in the café in case Lonnie does come here. And they will also watch the county roads."

"I'm going to post a sign," Jasmine said. "Outside the door of the café. It's supposed to tell how to get to my place so if Lonnie takes it, people will know where he's going."

The sheriff nodded. "We'll keep an eye on that, too."

Jasmine nodded. Everything was taken care of. "I guess I can concentrate on the pageant, then."

"You better," Carl said with a grin. "Because pulling in those deputies is the best advertising we could have done. By now the whole county knows we've got an angel flying in our pageant again. We could have a real crowd here. I'm thinking we should charge admission."

"Oh, we can't do that," Jasmine said. "I'm sure the church would never agree."

"They could use the money to finally buy some decent costumes, though," Wade said.

"The boys need to realize it's an honor to wear those bathrobes," Jasmine said. "They come from the community—with love."

Wade snorted. "You're welcome to try and

convince them of that. I'm taking care of it, but I've got one shepherd who was assigned a pink bathrobe. He may be scarred for life."

"Yes, well, that particular bathrobe was supposed to be for the girl's choir, but we didn't have enough shepherd costumes and—"

"Whatever you do, don't tell the shepherds that it's a girl's bathrobe," Wade said in mock horror and she laughed.

"I won't," she promised.

With that, the men went over to talk to the boys and Jasmine walked back to sing with the girls. Before she got there, though, Edith asked her to help carry in some new bathrobes that had been donated yesterday.

The sun was brighter this time when Jasmine stepped out of the barn. She looked up and noticed that the gray clouds from earlier in the day were giving way to light white clouds that scattered over a blue sky.

She walked with Edith over to Charley's pickup. Two boxes were sitting in the back of the pickup and Jasmine reached for one.

"Oh, we don't need to carry the boxes in," Edith said. "I thought we'd just pull out the bathrobes we need for today. Not everyone's here."

"Sure, that works," Jasmine said as she started

to pull one box closer to the end of the truck bed. There was a strip of bright purple showing in the other box and she put a hand out to that one until she realized it wasn't practical. She could see there were sensible colors in the box she was already pulling toward her.

"These will work good," Jasmine said as she opened the box flaps. "Lots of grays and beiges."

She looked up to see her friend studying her face.

"Why didn't you keep reaching for the purple robe?" Edith asked quietly. "You obviously liked it best."

Jasmine shrugged. "I just thought the other colors would be more suitable for the church's pageant."

It was silent for a minute.

"I notice you don't spike your hair as much anymore," Edith commented.

"Oh, that," Jasmine said as she reached up and ran her fingers through her hair to be sure it was under control. "It is a bit wild and—"

"Dear me," the older woman continued to stare at Jasmine. "I think I've led you astray."

"Huh?"

"I never noticed you stopped looking like you," Edith said, her words tumbling over each other. "You used to wear all those bright colors and, your hair, you even wore those red things in it sometimes."

"Streaks. They were streaks."

"I never meant to make you think that quiet colors were more appropriate in God's eyes," Edith continued in a rush. "Just because I wear them doesn't mean you need to. You don't have to be quiet to be a Christian."

Jasmine didn't know what to say and the older woman was still looking at her.

"And you hate dresses," Edith continued. "I should have realized something was wrong when you started wearing all those dresses."

"I only have three of them."

"And they're light gray, dark gray and beige," Edith said emphatically. "I bet you hate them all."

"Well, maybe a little."

"From now on, you need to dress like yourself. It's the only way things will work. Remember, God gave us peacocks and sunsets and rainbows."

"I can do peacock," Jasmine said with a grin.

"And let's bring that purple robe inside. Maybe we can find someone to play King Herod after all. I'm thinking he should be in the pageant even if he's just lurking in a corner somewhere acting like he's ready to pounce."

"I thought all of the roles were already assigned,"

Jasmine said as she pulled the box toward them that had the purple robe.

"Yes, but Wade needs a part," Edith said as they drew the robe from the box.

"I don't think Wade wants to be in the pageant."

"Which might just be the reason he should be. That boy has promise, you know. There's a reason God brought him back to us."

With that, Edith marched back into the barn with the purple robe draped over her arm.

Jasmine walked a little slower behind the other woman. She hadn't minded giving up the color in her wardrobe for God. At least, not much. She felt she should give Him something. Now, if she took the color back, flying as the angel was all she had left to give.

She opened the door and stood just inside the barn while Edith walked over to Wade with the purple robe. She couldn't hear what either one of them was saying, but Wade finally took the bathrobe and put it on so she supposed that was the answer. She wondered why God had brought that man back to Dry Creek.

She knew she should go back and sing with the girls, but instead she walked over to the group of boys that were with Wade. It was amazing how much control he had over the kids. He was so intent on talking to them he didn't even see she was there. She stood and looked at him. She wondered if he knew the boys idolized him.

Wade knew he was in trouble. He'd no sooner announced to the shepherds that he might play the role of Herod than they wanted to be in his army. Which meant they wanted weapons. They knew enough of the story to know that Herod had some kind of army and would have gotten rid of the wise men if he could have found them.

The shepherds were all in favor of anything that would cause trouble for the wise men that were rapidly becoming known simply as *them*.

"There is no us and them," he clarified. "The wise men are good men, too. And you don't need weapons during the Christmas pageant. Or, after, either. At your age, you don't need them at any time, really."

He heard someone clapping when he finished his brief speech and he knew it wasn't one of the shepherds so he turned to the side and saw Jasmine standing there. She'd fluffed her hair up and she tied the bottom of her T-shirt up in a way that made it look like a blouse.

"So you're the king?" she asked.

Wade felt a little foolish standing there in a

purple satin bathrobe that was too short for him and didn't tie right. "I said I'd be willing to stand in until Edith found someone else."

"He's going to die," one of the little shepherds announced solemnly to Jasmine.

"What?"

"He's a king without an army," the boy continued matter-of-factly. "Those wise men could take him—even without their donkey."

"I didn't say I don't have an army," Wade defended himself. "We just use our wits to protect ourselves."

"What's wits?" a shepherd asked.

"Brains." Wade pointed to his head. "My army thinks and plans."

"So you're a pacifist?" Jasmine asked, her voice ringing with delight.

"Uh." Wade felt trapped. "Not exactly. But I've never believed that it solves anything to just shoot things up."

"Like your grandfather does." Jasmine nodded like she understood.

Wade had never talked about his grandfather with anyone, but he wanted Jasmine to know. "He—I—ah—"

He was interrupted by a tug on his robe which was fortunate because he had forgotten he was surrounded by boys. He might want to tell Jasmine about the pain of his childhood, but he didn't want to announce it to the whole kindergarten world.

"Yeah?" he asked the boy.

"We could be a marching army," the boy finally said. "They don't have weapons."

"That's right. They don't," Wade said as he stepped a few feet away from the boys and motioned for Jasmine to follow him. He didn't want to wait until he drove her home to ask her because she might think it was just an add-on invitation. He wanted to ask her like it was important.

"Want to have dinner with me tonight?" he asked.

"The café is closed on Sunday."

"Oh," Wade said, and then pressed ahead bravely. "You could come have dinner with me and my grandfather, then. I'll clean the kitchen up and—"

"That would be great," Jasmine said.

"I'm not much of a cook, really, but I'll do my best."

Jasmine nodded.

"At least my grandfather's been pretty well-behaved," Wade felt compelled to add. "He says he stopped drinking a few months ago and I believe him. There aren't any empties around. And he hasn't been—"

Jasmine's face lit up. "I'll drive my motorcycle over."

"It's not a problem for me to come get you."

Jasmine looked like she was going to protest, but then she nodded even though the glow on her face dimmed.

The shepherds drew him back and, before he knew it, he was teaching them how to march in time with each other. They were hopeless at it, of course, but they were having fun and at least getting the concept of cooperation. If he was going to stay in Dry Creek, he wouldn't mind helping with the Sunday-school kids once in a while.

Whoa, he thought. Where had that thought come from?

Then he glanced across the barn at Jasmine singing with the girls and looked down at the boys gathered around his purple robe and he wondered how long he could manage to stay in this small town. He'd only thought to stay a few days, just long enough to do the job Carl had for him. But, according to the doctors, he wasn't ready to go back to his regular work yet, so if he wanted he could stay for another week or so. Even a month.

He skated around the thought of staying, giving it time to grow or die in his mind. He figured he'd come up with a dozen objections to the suggestion, but not one floated to his mind. He didn't even have a plant that would miss him back in Idaho Falls.

"Well, let's get to marching," Wade finally said, and his troops lined up and faced forward. He couldn't have been prouder of them if they had been officers of the law.

When the pageant practice was over, everyone drove down the road until they got to Dry Creek. Then they parked in front of the church and walked inside. Wade hadn't really intended to go that far with them, but he did. The morning had turned warmer and a nice fresh breeze was blowing. He surprised himself by walking up the steps with the others. If anyone asked him, he would say he was guarding Jasmine. But he knew he could do that by sitting on the steps of the church. He didn't need to go into the building for that.

He took an extra breath when he stepped through the door. So many of his childhood hopes had been born and then expired in this place. He'd learned to pray and then he'd learned his prayers didn't work. Now, he didn't know what to expect. The first thing he noticed was the inside of the church hadn't changed much since he'd been here over twenty years ago. The carpet might be new, but the wooden cross hanging behind the pulpit was still the same.

What did surprise him was that he was greeted like the prodigal son would have been at the party his father had given for him. The past years fell away. It seemed like everyone in the church came up and shook his hand. He knew some of it was because they had been reminded of him recently with the collection of money on his behalf, but they sure sounded sincere when they welcomed him home. He recognized most of the faces from his childhood even if he couldn't remember all of the names.

He didn't quite know what to do with so many well wishes so he was happy enough to have the piano signal that the service was ready to start. He let the words of the sermon wash over him without really listening. He wasn't ready to go quite that far as he tagged along with everyone. Besides, he was sitting next to Jasmine and he was captivated by the way several strands of her hair, down by her neck, were so wispy and, at the same time, reminded him so much of fine-tooled copper.

Before he knew it, church was over and people were heading to the back of the sanctuary for coffee. Wade was swept along with everyone else and, when he got there, Carl came over to give him a new update on the search for Lonnie.

Wade was happy for the contact. It reminded him of who he was.

Carl said a border-patrol officer thought he saw a man matching the description of the other escapee trying to drive through a checkpoint. The officer said there had been another man hunched down in the backseat of the car, but the two persons of interest had taken off before the officer could catch them. The officer knew they hadn't made it across the border into Mexico in that try as they'd turned back before he could give chase. But, he said, it wouldn't take long for two guys to slip through the border if they were determined.

"It has to be Lonnie and that other guy. So there's no need for you to guard Jasmine so closely," Carl said. "I'm sure that'll be a relief."

"Yeah," Wade said absentmindedly.

"Well, at least a relief for her," Carl amended his words with a laugh. "You know women—they need some space."

Everybody needed space. Wade knew that better than most. It should be fine if Jasmine rode her motorcycle over tonight. He went over and told her so and it made him feel like a hero to see the grin return to her face.

When Wade got back to his grandfather's place, he was astonished. The old man had actually cleaned the kitchen when Wade had been gone and set up the checkerboard on the table, hoping to play a game with him. Wade had forgotten the two of them used to play checkers before everything had gone so bad.

Wade agreed to a game, but said he could only play one since he'd invited company for dinner. They sat out on the porch so Wade could keep an eye on the road, but no one drove by and his grandfather actually won. Then he quietly called Wade by his own name.

"I thought you were going to call me Sonny forever," Wade said as he started putting the game pieces back in the box.

"Some days things are more clear than others," his grandfather said with a timid look at Wade. "I don't like to remember the past. It makes me ashamed of how I was. But, when Edith told me she'd asked you to come, I stopped drinking. I wanted to be sober so I could tell you something."

Wade blinked.

Then the old man added, "I'm sorry for the way I treated you. I should never have let things get that far out of control."

Wade had never thought he'd hear his grandfather say that much. He cleared his throat. He didn't quite know what to say. He wasn't ready to accept an apology for all that had happened. His grandfather had not been there for him when he needed him the most.

Then it hit him. "I'm sorry I wasn't here to see you were taken care of, either. I should have kept track of what was going on."

His grandfather reached his hand across the table and laid it on top of Wade's, but all he said was, "Now let's get ready for that dinner guest of yours. What's her name again?"

"Jasmine."

His grandfather nodded.

Wade knew he'd witnessed a miracle. Of course, tomorrow his grandfather might not remember a word he'd said. But he had stopped drinking. That was a start.

Tonight, Wade wanted to sit out on the porch with Jasmine and tell her what kind of a childhood he'd had. He doubted anyone could really know him unless he opened up about his isolation as a boy. It had been a long time since he'd cared about whether someone got to know him or not. Carl was probably the last real friend he'd made in his life and that was back in grade school. But Jasmine mattered.

He already had one strike against him in her eyes because he was a lawman. In fact, he probably had two strikes because of the church thing. His messed up childhood could be the final third strike and he'd be out of the game as far as she was concerned. But he still had to tell her.

He stood up. He'd bought some canned goods and bread when he drove through Billings on the way here. "This dinner I'm cooking needs to be good. Let's go see what we can find in the cupboard."

"I love sardines," his grandfather said with a grin.

That was the first time Wade could remember his grandfather making a joke. He looked at the older man carefully. Yeah, it had been a joke.

Wade spent the rest of the afternoon looking for a tablecloth and worrying about whether or not he could find glasses that matched. He knew he couldn't turn out a four-star dinner, but he was hoping for homey. He had several tins of a pretty good stew and a packet of English muffins. As long as all he had to do was heat the stew and toast the muffins, he'd do fine.

It felt good to be cooking for Jasmine and his grandfather. He sat down at one point and realized that, for the first time in decades, he was beginning to feel as if he might have a chance at a family.

Chapter Fourteen

Jasmine was living on the edge. She'd told her father that she was going over to the Suttons' for dinner and he'd given her a worried look. She wasn't sure if the look was because of Wade's grandfather's shotgun or Wade himself.

"Men can be dogs," her father finally said. She'd been in the hallway, putting on some lipstick, and then she'd come back into the kitchen to pick up her jacket. She'd taken Edith's words to heart and was wearing a vivid magenta blouse with her jeans. Plus some dangling silver earrings. And, her boots, of course. It felt good to be back in her own skin.

"Not all men, mind you," he added. "But some."

"I'm forty-three years old, Dad. I know about men."

Her father grunted. "I mean, that some men just

don't make commitments. They'll break your heart just because they can't help themselves."

"Ah." So her father saw it, too. She sat down next to him at the kitchen table and covered his hand with hers. "It's only dinner. He'll probably be gone right after Christmas."

"That's exactly what I'm talking about," her father said as he reached over with his other hand and patted hers. "You don't know each other very well yet. Wade was a good boy, but it's been a lot of years since he's lived around here. Sometimes when people move away, they find it hard to come back here after living in the big city."

"He lives in Idaho Falls. Not New York."

"Still," he said stubbornly. "I wouldn't want to see you get hurt."

Jasmine knew that, but she still got a lump in her throat when he said the words. Elmer hadn't been her first choice as a father, but he'd opened his heart to her without reservation.

She stood and kissed him on the top of the head. "Be sure and eat something for dinner yourself."

He nodded.

"I won't be late," she said as she walked over to get the jacket that she'd left on the chair by the refrigerator. Then she stopped by the counter and picked up her hostess gift.

She didn't know what to do when people invited her to dinner and things like that so a hostess gift made her feel more confident. That way, if she messed up on some other thing she was supposed to do, it went easier on her. Unfortunately, she'd used her last jar of jam going to the Walls'.

Her backup gift, two candles, didn't seem right. She already knew Wade didn't like to eat by candlelight and, given his grandfather's unsteady nature, a candle could cause a fire.

Finally, her mind had gone to chocolate and she'd grabbed an unopened bag of chocolate chips from the cupboard earlier. She'd gotten the chips one day when she'd convinced herself she would learn to make cookies. Now, with the red ribbon she'd tied on them, they managed to look festive.

"He better be buying you jewels," her father grumbled as he saw her pick up the bag of chips off the counter.

She laughed as she walked out the door.

The sun was starting to set and the air was colder than earlier in the day. Nothing made her feel more alive than slipping her helmet on her head and starting up her motorcycle. She was feeling good as she began the short drive over to the Sutton place.

Her father had already turned the lights on for

the cross. As the sun set, the hill turned black against a darkening sky and lit up the cross like a crystal chandelier hanging above everything. She half expected an Italian opera to begin, the cross gave the whole area that kind of dramatic style.

She drove slowly so she could enjoy the cross's beauty. Her father should leave the lights on all year around. She suspected the dramatic nature of the cross would turn lighter in the spring or summer. Maybe it would feel playful. It would be lovely to sit up beside the cross and have a midnight picnic.

She turned into the Sutton lane and was tempted to stop at the old pickup like the Covered Dish Ladies did, but she didn't. Lights were on in the house and it looked friendly.

Before she knew it, she was standing at the door, getting ready to knock when Wade opened it wide.

"Come in," he said.

Jasmine stepped inside and looked around. Someone had scrubbed the kitchen. And something smelled good. And—she looked up in surprise—Wade was looking nervous.

"I brought chocolate," she said as she held out the bag done up with the ribbon. "Well, just chips, really, but I wish it were jam."

Why was it that knowing he was nervous made her feel the same skittering way?

"Thank you. I like chocolate," Wade said solemnly as he accepted the gift.

Mr. Sutton came into the kitchen from the living room and smiled at her. "Jasmine, isn't it?"

She nodded and then looked at Wade.

"He has us figured out," Wade said. "Well, at least, he knows we're not my parents."

"Oh, that's good."

"I don't know." Wade gave a roguish smile. "He's not so likely to give me an order to kiss you."

Wade didn't wait for her to say anything, but he just held his hand out for her jacket. "May I?"

Jasmine handed him her jacket and her heart. She liked this lighthearted, flirtatious side of Wade. His grandfather asked if she'd like to sit down and she did. After a few minutes, the old man insisted he wanted to eat his dinner in the living room by the television so he left her alone in the kitchen with Wade.

She kept waiting for Wade to steal a kiss, but he seemed intent on being the perfect host instead. He brought her herb tea to drink while he finished toasting the English muffins. He brought her honey for the muffin before he brought a casserole dish filled with well-seasoned stew. By the time he had finished serving her, all of her earlier confidence was gone. Her father could have saved his breath warning her about men. Wade clearly wasn't ready to make a move of any kind.

"Did you ever get the fireworks out of Carl's car?" Wade asked when they were finished with their dinner. "I was going to help you and then I got all caught up with the boys and—"

"I thought I'd go over tomorrow and get it," Jasmine said as she folded her napkin beside her plate.

"I'll drive you," Wade said, nodding.

"I thought the Feds decided I was clean."

She regretted the words the minute they were out of her mouth. She was upset with him and she should have kept her mouth shut. They hadn't talked about *it* all evening. They'd just been a man and a woman sitting down to a meal together like it was a natural thing for them to do. But it wasn't natural, not for either of them. And he had not even tried to kiss her.

"They did," Wade agreed. "I just—"

Jasmine felt her heart break a little. "They may trust me, but you don't. Is that it?"

"No, I—" Wade swallowed. "I worry. That's all."

He looked at her with misery in his eyes. He might not trust her, but he clearly wasn't indifferent. She supposed it was hard for a lawman to open up to an ex-con. Maybe they both just needed more time.

"What time is good for you to pick me up?" she asked gently, and saw him relax.

"Maybe around ten. That'll give you time afterward to get ready for the pageant."

She nodded. Her father had been right to worry they were going too fast. She wondered if he was right about anything else. "You've been gone from your place in Idaho Falls for a while now. I suppose you can't wait to get back."

"The post office will only hold my mail for so long," he admitted.

That wasn't exactly a declaration of interest in staying here, she told herself. "You wouldn't want to miss any mail."

Wade grunted and then stood up. "A man needs more than mail in his life."

He took their plates to the sink and then went into the living room saying he needed to get something. He returned with a thick patchwork quilt made of blue and green squares.

"I thought we could sit outside and look at the cross awhile," he said. "My grandfather has a real good view from his porch."

"I bet you don't have anything like it in Idaho Falls."

"Not even close." He looked at her and his eyes grew warm.

Jasmine thought later that she would always re-member sitting on the porch with Wade that night. He wrapped that old quilt around them both and they talked for hours. In the darkness, they were equals. He wasn't suspicious of her and she wasn't defensive around him. He told her about his grandfather. She told him about her mother. They compared old pains and new dreams.

"Carl thinks I have a chip on my shoulder," he finally confided. "Told me so today."

"We all have problems of some sort."

"He said if I wanted to change, all I needed to do was do it."

Jasmine stopped breathing. She knew how important this was. "And do you? Want to change?"

Wade was silent for so long she didn't think he was going to answer. Finally, he said with a raw voice, "I don't think I can change."

Jasmine didn't stay for long after that.

Wade didn't blame her. He watched her walk out and get on her motorcycle and ride down the drive from his grandfather's house. She was right to leave him, of course. A man who could not change, not even when he wanted to, was only trouble and heartache for those around him.

He reminded himself that he needed to check

about that light she was expecting for her motor-cycle. The front light beamed out strong, but it was dangerous not to have a tail light. Maybe he'd have time to drive into Billings one day before he left. They should have every kind of lightbulb ever made in a town that size.

He wondered how he could trust her when he still had doubts. Of course, the doubts were shrink-ing, but that was only because the reports from the Feds seemed to clear her of any involvement.

Maybe once the pageant was over he could go get hypnotized or something. A man should be able to change if he wanted to and Wade had never had as much reason to change as he did now. There should be a hypnotist in Billings. If not, he'd go to Denver.

Then he realized he couldn't go anywhere until he made arrangements for his grandfather. And he'd promised some of the shepherds he'd take them someplace where they could see a fire engine. A month ago, he'd had no one to worry about, not even the usual trail of suspects he was doing surveillance on. And now, here he was, a man who was actually needed by someone who wasn't a fellow lawman.

Chapter Fifteen

It was Christmas Eve and Jasmine was looking out the windshield of her father's car. He was driving the Cadillac tonight, its white sides already dusted with snow before they left the house. The leather seats were cold enough to be uncomfortable and she could watch her breath in the light of the dashboard.

"You're sure you don't want me to stop and pick up Wade?" her father asked as he turned from their lane onto the main road. "He'd get a kick out of riding in this old car."

"No."

She'd made her decision. She had to cut Wade loose. She didn't want him to feel obligated to say he trusted her when he clearly didn't. Earlier, when he drove her over to the sheriff's to get that sack of fireworks, she had told him her father would take her to the pageant tonight and that's the way it should be. She was polite about it, of course. Not everyone was able to get over the fact that she was an ex-con. She could accept that. She didn't have to like it, but she could accept it.

Her father cleared his throat. "You're sure? 'Cause it'd be no trouble to stop and get him. He's right next door."

"I thought you didn't approve of Wade anyway."

"Well, but you seemed to like him and he's okay." Out of the corner of her eye, she saw her father turn to look at her. "Actually, I think he might be more than okay."

She shrugged and kept her eyes straight ahead. "He's the law."

She never should have forgotten that.

Her father was quiet the rest of the way. When he pulled up to the barn on the outskirts of Dry Creek, she counted twenty or so cars that were already parked around the place. That was a relief; the children were counting on a good audience for the pageant and it looked as if they were going to get one. More people would be coming later, of course. The snow had stopped and, when she stepped out of the Cadillac, she looked up and saw the stars. Dozens of pinpricks dotted the sky.

It was a lover's sky out tonight.

She forced her gaze back down to earth. A man, he looked like one of the hands from the Elkton Ranch, was standing on a tall ladder adjusting a light that was focused on the mural that had been painted on the barn last summer. She couldn't see his face because his gray Stetson kept it in the shadows.

Whoever he was, he had looped the cord for the light over the top of the high door that led into the loft where ranchers had stored their hay for many generations. The mural, with the figures of the men and women who'd lived in this area a hundred years ago, was a symbol of how connected this community was to its past and she felt good calling this place her home. She was even related to the past now that she knew her father was a Maynard, one of the early cattle families.

"If you need anything before you go up there, you just let me know," her father said as he pointed to the hayloft. The night was still cold, but the snow had stopped falling. "It'll be chilly in that angel costume. You'll be up higher than most people and there's that big door up there in the loft that's probably as drafty as all get-out even when it's closed."

"I'm wearing two pairs of socks," she said to comfort him.

She didn't add that she also had some string in her pocket to help her trail the sparklers from her feet. She'd checked with Edith and the barn would be fairly dark when she made her swing over it so the sparklers should make people catch their breath in wonderment when she passed. It was that initial gasp she was aiming for. That's what the shepherds would have done the first thing when they saw the angel, even before they fell to their knees.

She could almost see the looks on the shepherds' faces. She might not have a lover to view the stars with her, but she had no lack of friends and neighbors in this town. And she wanted to do something special for them to make this Christmas Eve feel holy.

The performers were supposed to arrive an hour early to be sure their costumes were on correctly, so Jasmine opened the door expecting to only see the kids who were in the pageant. But there was a crowd. Of course, the shepherds and the choir girls were all too young to drive themselves so their parents and other siblings had to come at the same time and no one would sit out in their cars in this weather. With nothing to do, the families all stood around, sipping cups of warm spiced cider and talking with each other.

Jasmine scanned the room, making sure Wade

wasn't there. She relaxed when she saw he wasn't. She laid her angel robe and the sack of fireworks by the ladder that led up to the hayloft. Then she saw Edith over by a refreshment table so she headed in that direction.

"Where's Wade?" Edith asked when she saw her. The older woman had some white towels in her arms and a frown on her face.

"I can help you," Jasmine offered. Why did everyone need Wade all of a sudden? He hadn't even been in the picture when they started practicing for the pageant.

"These are for the sheep," the older woman laid the towels in Jasmine's arms. "I haven't seen the shepherds and they're going to need them."

"Don't worry. I'll find them."

It didn't take her more than two minutes to do just that. The boys were huddled in a corner talking to their dogs.

"I have your towels," she said as she walked over to them.

They all looked up and then past her. "Where's Mr. Sutton?"

"You mean, Wade?"

They nodded.

"My dog doesn't feel so good," the smallest boy explained. "He needs some medicine."

"I don't know—" she began, and then stopped. The boys were looking at her with such trust on their faces. "Maybe I could get Charley for you. He's a vet."

This didn't seem to reassure the boys so she squatted down to be closer to them. "Charley takes care of all kinds of animals. Wade doesn't even have a pet."

She figured they could see from that which man would be better to call.

Jasmine saw the expression in the boys' eyes change from worry to near adoration as they looked behind her. She guessed what had happened before she saw the shadow on the floor in front of her.

"I have a donkey. That should count for something."

Wade.

Jasmine wanted to disappear. She figured he was looking at her about now so she refused to turn around until he left. She kept still, but the uneasy feeling of someone watching her continued.

Wade stood and watched Jasmine's back stiffen as the boys all scrambled to their feet. He wondered if she was going to face him. He wouldn't blame her if she didn't. She hadn't said they were through before they'd begun, but he could read body language.

He'd never been a quitter, but the thought of trying to change enough to be the man Jasmine wanted seemed as difficult as a blind man trying to jump across a deep ravine with nothing to guide him. It wasn't a lack of bravery; it was just an absence of any clue telling him how to do it. Even the blind man would only fall on his face if he tried to do the impossible.

When Jasmine didn't move, the donkey took a step forward. Wade pulled back on her halter. It said something about him that the only real friends he'd had as a boy had been this donkey and Carl—and he'd lied to Carl so the friend who'd known the truth about him was the donkey. And he only trusted her because she couldn't tell anyone else his secrets.

Wade knew he had lived his life in a small box that didn't require him to trust anyone or, since God always seemed to be pushing back into the picture, any Being, either. Wade believed what he saw and what he heard. He never worried about what his heart told him about people, because he went with his head. That's the way he'd been since he was a boy, but he knew it wasn't enough for someone like Jasmine.

So, he was going to turn around and go. But even though Jasmine didn't want to admire the donkey, the boys did.

"Can I touch it?" one of the boys asked as he stepped close.

"Her," Wade said as he patted the donkey's neck. "Her name's Jenny."

The donkey bowed her gray head until it was level with the boy. Then she looked at him with mournful eyes. She was a shameless beggar even if she couldn't smell oats. "Jenny's a little wet from the ride over here. Let her dry off first."

Jasmine finally turned around. "Just remember that she bites. Don't get close."

Then she looked up at Wade as if he was unfit to be around children—or donkeys, for that matter. "Does Edith know the donkey is here?"

Wade smiled. He would rather have Jasmine scolding him than ignoring him. "Edith told me to tie Jenny behind that curtain in the corner. It seems the wise men are going to ride her first for their chat with Herod and then she's going to be whisked away so Mary can use her for the big entrance."

"The two of you will be busy," Jasmine said as she stood up.

Wade watched as she lifted her arm and tentatively reached out to touch the donkey's coat.

"Actually, your father's going to keep track of her so I can play King Herod."

Just then Edith came walking through with a script in one hand and a little bell in the other. "It's time to get to your places. The pageant starts in ten minutes. Be sure you have your costumes all tied up securely."

"But my dog doesn't feel good," the shepherd boy said.

"Well, put him back with the donkey, then," Edith said. She was counting the shepherd boys as she spoke. Wade could see her lips moving.

The boy with the dog sat back in shock, "But the donkey *bites*."

Wade didn't know if the dog felt the shock from the boy and was reacting to it or if he heard the dismissal in Edith's voice, but he lifted his head from the floor, gave a vigorous yip, and stood up, miraculously healed.

"Attaboy," Wade said.

"Now, get your sheep towels on your dogs and go hide behind those boxes. Those are your hills," Edith said, directing them.

The older woman didn't see it because her eyes were already scanning the crowd looking for something else, but Wade proudly watched his shepherd boys line up and march their way to their hills. They could almost keep step with each other. Then, just before they disappeared behind the boxes, they all turned and saluted him.

Wade smiled and saluted them back.

"What was that about?" Jasmine asked.

"Oh, you know boys," he said. "They'd rather be soldiers than shepherds."

The boys were in mismatched bathrobes, but none of them were wearing pink. The shepherd who had been assigned the offending robe earlier was wearing Wade's old brown robe and looking very pleased with it, probably because the front pocket was partially torn off and no one would ever confuse it with a girl's robe. In addition, each shepherd had an old flour sack tied around his head to keep the desert sun off his face and sandals to keep the corresponding sand off his feet.

Jasmine nodded as she started to turn. "I guess I better get over to the hayloft and get my costume on."

"Before you do—did Carl reach you?" The sheriff had called Wade just before he left his grandfather's place to come here. "It looks like Lonnie is in custody. They caught two men trying to get across the border. They need to do fingerprints to be sure, but they think one of them is Lonnie."

"That's a relief."

"Not that it's for sure." Wade had never been one to have hunches or premonitions of any sort. But he had a buzzing in his head somewhere that made him unwilling to relax. Would Lonnie really go to Mexico?

Yesterday afternoon, the sheriff had dropped off copies of the transcripts from the inmate interviews that the Feds had done. None of the inmates remembered Lonnie ever mentioning Mexico. And just like the Feds had told them earlier, one inmate said that, during the last year, Lonnie had become freakishly obsessed with Jasmine.

"Of course, you can't let it bother you," Wade said. He knew inmate testimonies were notoriously unreliable. "Two deputy sheriffs are on their way here as we speak. And Carl will be on duty, too."

Jasmine nodded. "I better go."

"I'll be up to help with the wheel by the time you're ready to go."

"Charley can help me," Jasmine said.

Wade knew he should let her go. When he finished with his bit as King Herod, he could guard her from the steps leading up to the hayloft and she never even needed to know he was there. He'd just seen the deputy sheriffs step inside the barn so he knew they'd be watching the entrances. There was no reason for him to worry. It's just that he didn't want to miss seeing Jasmine's face when she swung back to the hayloft after she made her pronouncement to the shepherds.

"It won't hurt to have another pair of eyes watching that wheel," Wade said, keeping his voice casual.

Just then they both heard the ring of a bell. That was Edith's signal that everyone should take their places.

Wade was glad Jasmine went rushing off to the hayloft without telling him definitely that she didn't want him there. It wasn't that he was shy about pushing his way in where people didn't want him. He did that all the time with the bad guys. But he wouldn't do it with Jasmine.

The strange thing was, he wanted Jasmine to trust him. She'd never said that her old boyfriend, Lonnie, had been overbearing, but reading those inmate interviews made him think it was a good guess. If Lonnie had been the kind to push her around, Wade wanted to give her plenty of room.

The sounds of footsteps and whispers gradually wound down as the audience took their seats in the folding chairs around the edge of the barn. Wade hadn't been to one of these pageants since the disastrous night when he'd been the angel, but he felt the peace of it all settle into his bones.

Edith had marked off a place for him to stand in a shadowed area near where the wise men passed by. Wade took one last look at the audience and walked over to his post. His last thought before the pageant began was to wonder who in the audience had bought a purple satin bathrobe a decade or so ago. And what they thought now that it was being used in the pageant to help portray a king.

This was what being part of a community was like, Wade thought to himself. It was remembering the kids and the traditions of one's home even when shopping. He wondered if he'd ever belong to a place like that.

Chapter Sixteen

Jasmine paused at the foot of the ladder leading up to the hayloft, her gown and sack in her hand. The lights had just dimmed in the barn and everyone was quiet. A sudden cold breeze blew in from somewhere and she pulled her collar a little more firmly around her neck. Even with that, she was chilled.

She looked over the audience that lined the walls of the barn and wondered how many people here were lonely tonight. Not many, she guessed. She saw a chipped-toothed toddler being held in his mother's lap. Even the men from the Elkton Ranch were sitting together and focused on the pageant. Then the spotlight was gradually turned up and the narration began.

"Jesus was born in the town of Bethlehem in

Judea, during the time when Herod was king," a man's voice came out over the microphone. Jasmine knew it was a recorded voice, but it was mellow and it pulled her into the story.

She wondered if Bethlehem was as small as Dry Creek. If it was, she could understand how difficult it would have been to find housing for a crowd of people. It would be like when they held their infrequent rodeos here. Surely they would have found room for a pregnant woman, though. Edith would have seen to it if Mary and Joseph turned up in Dry Creek. They'd be in her own bed if necessary.

The spotlight went over to King Herod as the narrator continued. Wade's purple satin bathrobe was too short and his crown was made out of a painted coat hanger. He'd pushed his jeans up to his knees and he wore plastic sandals. But, as he stood there, his back militarily straight and his eyes scanning the distance as though looking for enemies, he truly seemed like a powerful king of old.

Her eyes could have watched Wade all night, but the wise men shuffled into the scene. They were leading the donkey who had saddlebags tossed over her back. The bags were stuffed to overflowing with plastic gold beads and one particular string was swinging back and forth over the donkey's side and the animal didn't seem to like it.

If that string of beads broke, they could repeat the disaster of the pageant Wade remembered where beads rolled everywhere and people stumbled on stage. Jasmine was tense until she noticed Kind Herod casually tuck the string of beads back where it belonged while the wise men whispered together, one of them pointing up at the heavens.

As the wise men continued on their course, King Herod slipped out of sight through one of the side doors of the barn. If it had been anyone else, she would think he was leaving. But, given who he was, she was pretty sure the king was making one final check outside to be sure Lonnie was nowhere around. Even when the Feds told him he could ease up, he wouldn't.

Jasmine blinked a few times. It was too bad that he couldn't trust her.

Oh, well. She decided it was time for her to go and get ready. She'd seen Charley move up the ladder ten minutes ago so he'd be in place. Her cardboard wings were already up in the loft. She looked in her fireworks sack to be sure she'd included a lighter for the sparklers.

Then, she turned to the ladder and began the

climb. The ladder was a permanent part of the barn and it had nice wide rungs, which was good because she had her robe and the fireworks in one hand and only had the other hand to hold herself steady as she went up the ladder.

The hayloft was about fifteen feet off of the main floor and, about halfway up, Jasmine turned to look back down at the stage. She was holding one rung and had her feet on another. Mary and Joseph were making their journey, with Mary riding on the donkey and Joseph leading them. By now, the donkey wasn't even bothering to look at all the people sitting around watching her. She seemed more interested in the fake little town she saw in the distance. Jasmine wondered if someone had thought to put oats in the stable.

Jasmine turned back to the ladder and continued. Her father had been right, she decided, about it being colder as she went higher. She wondered if that cowboy checking the outside light earlier had left the hayloft door open when he climbed down.

Her head came up inside the hayloft and she was facing toward the back of the area. Which meant she could see that the door was open. She was surprised Charley hadn't closed it, but he was probably too preoccupied with the wheel. Even in the dark, she could feel the wind blowing around tiny pieces of hay. The bales seemed to shed for some reason she didn't understand. Every time she'd been up here it seemed like there was more hay dust than before.

"Charley," she said as she threw the fireworks sack and her white robe onto the floor next to the opening and braced her arms to lift herself completely up into the hayloft. She was surprised when he didn't answer, but it flashed through her head that he might have gone down to say something to Edith. After all, the angel wasn't on for another ten minutes—longer if the girls' choir didn't increase their speed as they sang "It Came Upon a Midnight Clear."

Jasmine was on her knees by the time she could look around. The stacks of hay bales looked taller than she remembered. And there were fewer of the stacks. The angel wings weren't where she'd left them, but she could see them leaning against a different stack of bales. Someone had been moving the bales around, which was an odd thing to do. She wondered what Charley thought he was doing. At his age, he had no business moving anything that heavy.

And then she saw the Stetson hat, sitting on the floor next to the wheel. It was dark and shadowy in the loft, but she figured the gray hat must belong to the cowboy who'd been fixing the light outside. She stood up and started to take a step toward the hat, but then she stopped. Ranch hands generally had two hats, one for dress and one to wear when they worked. That hat looked new. Something was wrong if a cowboy left his dress Stetson in the middle of the floor like that. This place hadn't been swept up here in years.

Jasmine swallowed her panic. She tried to soundlessly turn to leave the loft when she heard a click. It was just a little sound. But she knew all too well what a gun sounded like when the hammer was pulled back with intent to fire.

"Don't worry. It's me," a man whispered, and her mouth went dry.

She had to turn around and face her past. "Lonnie?"

Her ex-boyfriend stood up behind some hay bales. It was dark and he was both thinner and older than she remembered him, but she would have known his face anywhere. His hairline was pushing back from his forehead and his eyes darted around in a way they had not used to do, but his grin—she would know that grin anywhere.

"It's me, baby," he said. "I came to get you."

"You're supposed to be in prison." Jasmine didn't want Lonnie to know there were deputy sheriffs downstairs waiting in case he came here. Of course, she realized as her heart sank, the deputies would be checking people as they came into the barn. They'd never think of a ladder up to the hayloft.

"You know there's no prison strong enough to stand between the two of us." Lonnie's eyes looked a little wilder than she remembered. He lowered his voice in what probably passed for romantic with him. "We're meant to be together. I missed you, baby."

Lonnie took a step out from behind the short stack of bales. That's when Jasmine saw the guns. He had one in his hand and another one stretching the waistband of his jeans.

"How'd you get here?" she stalled.

Lonnie grunted. "I heard about the pageant in Miles City. Some guys said there was a good-looking red-haired angel who was new to town and she had just found her father. I knew it had to be you. Sounds like you've got a good thing going here."

"What do you want from me?"

"I want you to come with me," Lonnie said as if he was surprised she'd have to ask. "I got the ladder set up and everything. Even got a pickup truck parked outside with clean plates and a full tank of gas."

Jasmine's heart stopped. "I can't go with you."

Lonnie's grin ended. "We don't have time for you to play hard to get. I came all this way to find you. You're coming with me."

"Please, just leave. If you go quick enough, no one will even know you've been here."

"That old man will know," Lonnie said as he jerked his head toward a stack of bales near the one he'd been hiding behind. "He's out now, but he'll come to unless I—"

Lonnie held up the gun.

"No," Jasmine gasped. "You've done enough damage. You can't—"

Lonnie just stood and looked at her. "You've changed."

Jasmine nodded. "Of course, I've changed. What we had all those years ago wasn't a life."

"It was good enough for me," Lonnie said, and she could feel the chill in his voice. "Are you saying you're too good to go on the road with me now that I busted out of jail to come get you?"

"I'm not saying anything. I'm just asking you to leave here."

Lonnie walked closer to her. "You got yourself another man, don't you? That's it, isn't it?"

Jasmine forced herself not to take a step backward. Lonnie enjoyed making people afraid.

So she stood there even when he was close enough that she could smell his sweat. "There's no man."

"Maybe not, but there's something." Lonnie studied her silently.

The girls' choir was almost finished with singing their songs. Jasmine should be putting her wings on. If the angel didn't show, people might come up to see what was wrong and someone else could get hurt. Then Jasmine heard a soft moan from behind the hay bales. She didn't want Lonnie to know Charley was regaining consciousness.

"You should turn yourself in," Jasmine said quickly. The only way she knew to ensure Lonnie's attention stayed on her was to get him angry.

"You'd like that, wouldn't you?" Lonnie growled. "You making a fool out of me?"

Jasmine braced herself for a slap to the face. But then they heard footsteps on the ladder.

"Who's that?" Lonnie hissed as he stepped away from her.

"I don't know."

Then a man called out, "Jasmine."

"It's him, isn't it?" Lonnie said as he took a few steps sideways to hide behind another short stack of bales. When he was almost there, he slid his extra gun across to her. "Pick that up and order your boyfriend to leave."

"I'm not going to do that," Jasmine said. Why did it have to be Wade coming up here? "Not even if you shoot me."

"Oh, I'm not going to shoot you." Lonnie gave a low chuckle. "I'm going to shoot him." He paused. "Dead center. He deserves it for messing with my woman anyway."

"No—" Jasmine whispered.

"And you better be convincing," Lonnie added as he slid into the darkness behind the bales. "Or I'll shoot him just for the fun of it."

Jasmine bent down to pick up the gun. The metal was cold and heavy in her hands. Years ago, Lonnie had taught her how to shoot a gun so she knew how to aim and fire with the best of them. She raised the gun so Lonnie could see she was taking his threat seriously. Then it occurred to her. It wouldn't be hard for her to be convincing in this little drama; it's what Wade had been expecting all along.

She could see the top of the lawman's head as he came to the end of the ladder. She only saw the back of his head now, but he'd need to pull himself up into the loft with his arms and then he'd turn around and see her. Her heart was pounding and she couldn't think of the words to pray. All that went through her mind was, *Please, God. Please, God. Please, God.*

Then it all became clear. *Please God, let Wade think his worst. Make him agree to leave. Let him be safe.*

Jasmine forced back the tears she felt. She needed to play her part well.

Wade pushed himself up the rest of the way into the hayloft. He felt an itch on his neck and thought some hay dust must have filtered down while he was climbing up the ladder. He'd taken his Herod robe off and had to catch one of the wayward sheep and return it to the shepherds so he hadn't gotten here as quickly as he'd expected. Charley would have Jasmine ready to go, though.

A faint sob alerted him. Someone had bit back the sound almost before it was out of their mouth, but he heard it. He was still facing toward the open hayloft door and he saw the short spokes of the ladder that rose just inches above the bottom of the opening.

He let the message of that ladder sink in. His back was already to whoever was in the loft and they hadn't knifed him or shot him thus far. He could start climbing down and they might never aim for him. But Jasmine was here. And Charley.

Wade swung his legs around so he could stand. These days that motion usually made him wince in pain, but he didn't even give it a passing thought. He turned around slowly so he wouldn't startle anyone and finally faced the gun.

He hadn't expected Jasmine to be the one, but she held the pistol steady and aimed at his heart.

They just looked at each other for a few seconds. It gave Wade time to orient himself. The hayloft was full of shadows, more so because of the spotlight shining in the other part of the barn. There were stacks of bales here and there and they'd been moved since he'd been up here yesterday.

"Is something wrong?" Wade finally asked just to give Jasmine space to talk.

Maybe if she said something she would give him a clue about what was happening. Someone must have a gun aimed at her, he finally decided. She stood there completely stiff.

Wade moved his eyes slightly, trying to decide which hay bales hid the person who threatened her. He didn't want that person to know he was looking so he was careful not to move his head.

He looked at Jasmine. It was so dark he couldn't see her eyes. He could see the strain on her face, though.

"I want you to leave," she said, her voice hard and flat.

For a second, it occurred to him that he didn't

really *know* there was anyone else in the hayloft. He couldn't see or hear or smell anyone. And then, just as quickly, he realized the reason he knew she was innocent was because he trusted her. *He, Wade Sutton, trusted someone.* In his heart, he was one hundred percent positive Jasmine would never hold a gun on anyone like she was doing now—not unless there was someone else here who was a whole lot more deadly.

It was Lonnie, of course. It had to be.

"I came to help with the wheel," Wade said, sounding as close to a witless idiot as he could. "You need help with the wheel."

"What I need is for you to go back down those stairs and leave me alone," Jasmine repeated.

Wade took a step closer to her.

"No," Jasmine gasped.

Wade noticed the quick flick of her eyes as they went to the hay bales in the middle on his right. So that's where the person was.

"You've got to leave," Jasmine said again, her voice rising a little and sounding desperate.

Wade was measuring the distance from the hay bale to him. It was too far away to risk it. If Lonnie had a gun trained on her, Wade needed to be closer to block it. If he could just get himself a few feet closer.

"I'll leave when I get the wheel set," Wade said, trying to sound normal. "I think one of the spokes needs some grease." He gestured to his pocket. "I've got some in here. Just the thing."

Wade took a small step farther into the hayloft. He didn't want to push too quickly and make anyone nervous. Then, as he started to take another step, he heard something. *Oh, no.* Behind him was the sound of boyish voices and light feet.

He knew Jasmine could see what was happening because he saw the horror reflected on her face.

"No. Go back," she whispered.

Wade turned around in time to see two of the shepherd boys pop their heads up through the opening into the hayloft. Fortunately, they were still facing toward the back wall.

"Go back down those stairs," Wade said. "Don't turn around. Don't come up here. Just—"

Wade heard the rustling of hay off to his side.

"Tell them to come up," the man said, and Wade looked over. So this was Lonnie. The man continued, "They've seen too much."

"They haven't seen anything," Wade said fiercely. "One of them is just worried about his dog. They'll go back down." He softened his voice. "They aren't even going to turn around, are you, fellas?"

Wade saw the little heads shake their heads vigorously.

"I said to tell them to come up here," Lonnie almost screamed.

Wade took a deliberate side step which caused Lonnie to twist and look over at him.

"Leg pain," Wade said with feeling in his voice. He noticed the little heads had known who to obey and were scrambling down the ladder. He wasn't sure what they'd think because they hadn't seen anything and had only heard two men arguing. Hopefully, any adult they talked to would know how to make sense of it all.

"You'll have a dose of real pain if you don't watch it," Lonnie said as he jabbed his gun in Wade's general direction. Then he turned to Jasmine. "We better get out of here, baby. Everything's going to bust loose any minute."

Jasmine stood rooted to where she stood. Wade figured she had to have heard Lonnie. But she wasn't moving.

"No point in looking at Romeo there," Lonnie said as he went over and snapped his fingers by Jasmine's ears. "I'm not going to be too happy if you get us caught again. When I say we need to get moving, I mean it."

Wade couldn't get to Lonnie, not with Jasmine

in the range of fire. The only escape he saw was for Lonnie and Jasmine to leave. With Lonnie thinking they were safe. Then he could follow them and take Lonnie when he wasn't around Jasmine. It wasn't a good plan, but Wade didn't know what else to do. Lonnie looked as if he'd be happy to shoot anyone.

"Go with him," Wade whispered to Jasmine.

She started to move toward the ladder Lonnie had used to come inside. The man himself was crowding close behind her.

Finally, Wade saw his chance. He waited for Jasmine to be far enough down the ladder that Lonnie couldn't shoot at her. Then he stepped close, plucked Lonnie up by the collar, and half swirled the man around so he could give him a solid punch to the stomach. The man not only dropped his gun, he bent over trying to get enough air in his lungs.

Bringing down a lowlife was one of the joys of being a lawman, Wade said to himself, as he pulled Lonnie back up. But then, as he thought of what Lonnie could have done, his blood turned cold. The stakes in a fight had never been so high. What if Lonnie had hurt Jasmine?

Wade had rescued countless people from harm and he'd cared about each of them. But to have Jasmine hurt? It couldn't happen.

Chapter Seventeen

Jasmine heard Lonnie's grunt, but she kept scrambling down the ladder anyway. She didn't have a coat and the air was cold. She'd have to get a lawyer, she thought to herself. There was no way to explain what had happened up there, not when Wade had seen her act like she was Lonnie's partner again. She wasn't sure it would be considered a forced situation that she had held a gun on Wade or not. He was a lawman. She could receive an even longer sentence for tonight than she'd served for the robbery all those years ago.

She heard noises at the top of the ladder and glanced up to see Wade standing in the open loft door. Behind him were shadows, but the outside light showed him clearly. His legs were braced for balance. His white shirt was askew on his shoulders like he'd been in a fight. His dark hair was tousled and his eyes so intense they took her breath away.

"Jasmine—" He held on to the door and leaned out a little before saying quietly, "Drop your gun."

Until then, she had forgotten she was still carrying it. Just then she heard a sound to her left and Sheriff Wall raced around the corner of the barn, dressed in his official sheriff uniform and holding his weapon in his hand.

"Drop the gun," Carl commanded. His voice didn't waver. "Now."

Jasmine forced her hand to release the gun and she let it fall to the ground. She wanted to cover her eyes, but she couldn't. She had to keep climbing down. "I'm not armed."

She glanced up and saw that Wade was no longer standing in the hayloft doorway. She felt as if her heart had cracked wide-open. He would always see her as a criminal and she would always remember him looking down on her asking her to drop her weapon. Maybe Lonnie would tell the truth about what happened in the hayloft. Maybe the courts would decide she was innocent. But Wade would always be suspicious of her.

She stumbled on the bottom rung of the ladder and felt the shadows enfold her. The spotlight was focused on the mural higher up on the barn wall and she was grateful to be in the dark. Her feet no sooner touched the ground than she felt the ladder shake. She looked up and Wade was crawling down the ladder faster than she had.

"Easy on the trigger, Carl," he called as he started down.

Jasmine put her hands behind her neck. She knew Carl hadn't asked for the arrest position, but she didn't want any misunderstandings. She turned away slightly so she wouldn't have to face Wade directly when he talked to the deputy sheriff.

"Your suspect's upstairs," Wade announced when he reached the ground and stepped off the ladder. "I tied him up with my belt, but that won't keep him forever."

Carl nodded. "One of the other deputies is on the way up to the loft." He used his head to point at Jasmine. "I had a hunch about checking this ladder and I ended up surprising this one here."

Jasmine winced. *Lord,* she began, but no words followed. When did she become "this one" to her friend, Carl?

"That's not the way it went down," Wade said as he stepped over to Jasmine.

The warm sound of his voice encouraged Jasmine to look up at his face. He was standing closer to the light and his face was visible. She looked carefully to see if he had any bruises after his fight with Lonnie. There were none, but then she noticed his eyes. She'd expected to see pity or condemnation. Instead, all she saw was a steady regard. Kindness flooded his eyes and there was something deeper that made the tension in her slide away.

"You don't need to keep your hands up," Wade said as he reached up and guided her arms down to her sides. Her skin felt warm everywhere he touched it.

"Hey," Carl protested. "She had a gun. It's right there on the ground where she dropped it."

Wade turned to the sheriff and then back to Jasmine with a smile. "I know she had a gun, but she didn't shoot me. That's got to say something."

"Well, that doesn't mean—" Carl started to sputter and then he glared at Wade. "What's gotten into you anyway? You've been saying all along that she's guilty. Now that we know she is, you turn into her defense counsel."

Wade ran his finger down Jasmine's cheek and she felt safe for the first time since this whole thing started.

"The thing is…" Wade kept looking at Jasmine even though he spoke loud enough for

Carl to hear. "I was wrong the whole time. She's not guilty."

Jasmine searched the eyes looking into hers.

"Well, I don't know," Carl said with a frown, but he did lower his gun. Then he stepped over to Wade's side. "I suppose you've got some evidence to support your theory."

"Not a bit of it," Wade said.

"I hope you're not going to say you have a hunch."

"No." Wade looked up at him finally. "It's no hunch. I have no evidence. I just know."

"Now you're just freaking me out," Carl said, and then he looked at Jasmine. "What'd she do? Give you something funny to drink?"

Wade shook his head, but he didn't get much chance to say anything else because a whole crowd of people were crashing around the corner now.

At least, it felt like a crowd of people to Jasmine.

"Are you okay?" Her father was leading the pack and he headed straight for her. Wade stepped aside to let her father through and he wasn't satisfied until he wrapped his arms around her.

"I'm fine," Jasmine tried to speak, but her words were muffled as her father crushed her face into the front of his wool coat. She let him hold her for a second and then she started to squirm. "Can't breathe."

With that, her father loosened his arms and stepped back a little. He was blinking furiously and frowning. "I'm getting you pearls for Christmas, too. To go with your diamonds."

Jasmine gave a half laugh. "No one wears pearls with diamonds."

"Then you'll have to take one of the cars," her father said emphatically. "I have to give you something more."

"You already did," Jasmine said as she hugged him back.

She expected to see Wade standing off to her right because that's where he'd stepped when her father came barreling toward her. But, when she turned, he wasn't there. She looked over the others gathered around and didn't see him. Linda was there. Barbara Wall, looking stricken, was standing next to the donkey. Then Jasmine noticed that Barbara's son was one of the shepherds riding on the donkey. A couple of the Elkton Ranch men were there looking as if they were ready to defend anyone who needed it. But the sheriff and Wade had both gone.

Jasmine figured that meant she was free to go. She stepped away from her father and the chill of the evening made her shiver. She hadn't realized it was this cold. She looked up and noticed the sky was totally black. Clouds had closed off the stars. Where had Wade gone?

"Let's get you inside," her friend Linda said as she stepped forward, put an arm around her shoulders, and started to guide her back to the barn entrance. Everyone else followed them, including the boys on the donkey.

"The pageant," Jasmine remembered with a gasp when she saw the open door of the barn. "We didn't finish the pageant."

"That's okay," Linda said as she kept leading her inside the barn. "Don't worry about anything."

Jasmine's started to shake. She barely made it over the doorway before she started to tremble.

Linda looked up and called someone.

Before Jasmine had time to think, Wade was leading her to a place at the side of the door and putting his coat over her shoulders. She barely had time for the warmth to set in before he had enfolded her in a hug that was almost as strong as her father's.

"Breathe deep," he said as he held her close to him. "Take it in. Breathe it out."

She could smell the scent of him. He must have used some pine-scented soap. She kept taking deep breaths and felt the press of his lips against the top of her head. His arms supported her and after a few minutes she felt her heartbeat match his.

They just stood together.

Finally, Wade stepped far enough away so that he could look down at her. "Are you all right now?"

She nodded.

He drew her back to him for another hug.

By then Jasmine noticed that everyone in the barn was stirring. People were walking here and there, shifting to make room for something. Then she saw that the deputies were bringing Lonnie down the inside ladder.

Lonnie looked scuffed up, but when he reached the floor, his eyes began looking over the people in the barn until he found her. The deputies, one on each side of him, marched him to the door. Lonnie stared at her the whole time and, when he passed by, he suddenly lunged at her.

"I'll get you," he snarled as the deputies pulled him back. "Nobody messes with Lonnie Denton, not even you."

Jasmine didn't say a word; she just sank into Wade's protective shoulder.

"Don't give him another thought," Wade whispered to her as the deputies marched Lonnie out of the barn.

After Lonnie left the building, Carl started down the ladder, too. He was helping Charley make the steps.

"Oh," Jasmine said as she walked toward the two men. "I forgot about Charley."

She could see a bruise on Charley's forehead, but otherwise he looked as if he was okay. "You need to have a doctor look at your head."

She saw Edith making her way over to Charley from the opposite side of the barn.

Wade was right behind her, his eyes on Carl. "Didn't we tell you to bring the paramedics?"

Carl snorted. "Who would think we'd need them? This is a church pageant."

"We're going to drive him to the clinic in Miles City," one of the Elkton ranch hands said.

"Not without me you're not," Edith said as she reached up to touch her husband's face.

"Of course, not without you," the ranch hand agreed. "I'll bring the pickup around."

Charley turned to look around while he waited. His wrinkled face was pale, except for his bruise. His eyes went to Jasmine. "I told the sheriff what happened. I think I heard everything he said to make you hold that gun on Wade here."

The older man gave a nod to Wade. The crowd had grown silent as Charley spoke and his cracked, hoarse voice carried throughout the barn.

Even though Wade had known there was an explanation for Jasmine's actions, he was glad to know Charley had heard Lonnie make the threats.

Trusting Jasmine was getting easier all of the time. He turned to her. "You know you're clear of the law if he said he'd shoot you if you didn't hold that gun on me."

"Oh, but he didn't say that," Charley protested. He was almost out the door, but he turned back to look at Wade. "He threatened to shoot *you* if she didn't do what he said."

"Me?" Wade felt his whole world shift.

"She wouldn't do it when she thought he'd just shoot her," Charley finished his words, and exited the barn.

Wade could only stare after him. He thought he was doing so well to trust Jasmine without seeing proof that she was innocent. He'd never even imagined that she was doing what she did to keep *him* alive.

Something of Wade's astonishment stirred the other people standing around. He couldn't move. He just looked down at Jasmine in amazement.

Then someone started the sound system again and the music to "Silent Night" began to flow over everyone in the barn. People started humming, but soon everyone gathered their voices together to sing the old carol with quiet reverence. Wade felt resentments he'd held on to for years being washed away as he listened to the simple words being sung by his old neighbors.

When the song was finished, everyone stood quietly. Finally, Pastor Matthew stood and suggested they share a Christmas benediction. Wade bowed his head. He told himself it was just so no one could see him wiping away a stray tear. Even with all of the bowed heads, he reached out and took hold of Jasmine's hand so they could hear the benediction together.

All of Wade's past thoughts about God and love and other people tumbled around in his head and in his heart. He'd been wrong. For all those years, he'd been wrong. He could barely take it in.

Chapter Eighteen

Frost covered the windows on Christmas morning. Jasmine didn't even notice, though, as she sat by the sparsely decorated tree in her father's living room and recited to herself the many ways in which she'd been blessed. She was no longer in prison. She was a child of God. She'd almost been the angel in a church pageant. She had a home and a father who loved her.

She stopped herself. It should not matter so much that Wade was going back to Idaho Falls later today. He'd told her as much last night—his words choppy and confused—but she should have expected it. The bad guy had been caught and there was no one else who needed to be followed in Dry Creek. She'd always known he was a loner.

"We can open the presents later if you want,"

Elmer said as he brought two cups of hot cocoa into the living room and handed one to Jasmine. He was in his bathrobe. "I'm happy to just sit here for a while."

Jasmine glanced over at her father. "You're not coming down with something, are you? I thought you couldn't wait to give me all your presents."

She pulled her gray sweater more closely around her. She knew Edith expected her to wear bright colors now, but the gray was all she could manage today.

"Yeah, well," her father cleared his throat. "I've been thinking about that ham I got us for Christmas dinner. It's so big that we'll be eating on it for a month of Sundays if we don't do something."

Jasmine shrugged. "We both like soup. Bean and ham is good."

Her father nodded as he set his cup on the coffee table. "We could always invite our neighbors over to share it. I mean, if we didn't want to have to eat as much soup."

"What?"

Her father kept nodding. "Last night made me think it's time to end this feud I have with Clarence Sutton. From all I hear, he's just an old man now. What's the fun in besting an old man?"

"I—ah—" Jasmine sputtered.

"Old Clarence and I, we just need to compromise with each other."

Jasmine finally swallowed. "Well, that would be commendable. Very mature. In a good way."

"It'd be all right with you?" her father asked and she knew what he wanted to know. "If we ask them over for dinner?"

"Wade will probably be gone by then," she said. "He'll want to at least make it to Billings tonight. But I'm sure Clarence would be very pleased to come."

"Oh."

Jasmine smiled at her father. "I know what you're trying to do and it's sweet, really, but—"

Just then they heard the sound of an engine driving up their lane. Jasmine had to stand up on tiptoes to look through the upper window because the panes on the bottom were covered with frost. Her father went in the kitchen.

It was Wade, driving the old pickup of Clarence's, who was coming to visit.

"It's him," her father announced as he came dancing back into the living room and grabbed the largest present under the tree. "Quick, open this."

Jasmine ran her fingers through her hair. She didn't have time to open presents. Not when she looked like a natural disaster.

Finally, her father tore the paper off of the package himself. "Put this on."

Her father pulled a long winter coat out of the box. It was a deep forest green with raglan sleeves and square brass buttons down the front. There was black velvet piping around the collar and the cuff.

"It's beautiful." Jasmine took off the gray sweater.

"Quick," her father said as he opened up the coat, and when she lifted her arms, slid it on for her.

Jasmine was all buttoned up by the time she heard the knock on the door.

"I'll be in the living room," her father said as he nodded his head toward the kitchen. "You go ahead and answer."

Jasmine nodded. She wondered if Wade needed something like a cup of sugar or something. Or maybe he wanted to be sure the Covered Dish Ladies would continue cooking for his grandfather once he had left.

Whatever it was, she'd agree quickly so he'd be gone just as fast. She took a breath and opened the door.

Jasmine felt all her resolve drain out of her when she looked up at his face. All she could do was stare. His eyes were smiling at her in a way that made her want to smile back.

* * *

Wade had never seen a more perfect Christmas angel. The green of the coat made Jasmine's hair glow with a brighter copper color. She had some heat in her face and it gave her just the right pink to her complexion. Her hair wasn't spiked or curled, either. Instead it tumbled around her face in joyous confusion. And something swelled in his throat, making it hard for him to speak. He was in love.

"Do you need something?" she asked. "Butter? Sugar? Milk?"

Wade shook his head. "I wanted to give you a Christmas present, that's all."

He watched the disbelief flicker across her face.

"It's not much," he added. "At least not in terms of money."

Jasmine stepped back and let him into the kitchen before closing the door again.

Wade had been nervous all morning. He'd gone to bed realizing he didn't have a Christmas present for Jasmine and there were no stores within a hundred miles that would be open on Christmas day. Just yesterday, it hadn't seemed important. But last night, when his heart broke wide-open, he knew he wanted to give her a present. And not just any present; he wanted something worthy of the emotions that were running riot inside him.

It had taken Wade a while to remember his mother's old jewelry box that was lying with the magazines up in the hayloft of his grandfather's barn. He'd been up there once since he'd been back to check on the magazines and he'd seen the small wooden box.

His mother never had much jewelry, of course. There'd been no money for things like that. But she did have one piece. It was a silver chain necklace with a small amber teardrop on it that she had obviously treasured since she was wearing it in every picture Wade had seen of her.

He didn't have a way to polish the chain, but he did carefully lay it out when he went out to the barn to get it.

Wade didn't have a small gold box like a proper jeweler would have so he finally wrapped the necklace in a piece of tinfoil. At least that was bright and shiny. "I used the ribbon you had on the package of chips. I hope you don't mind."

Jasmine took the present, holding it as if it would disappear any moment.

"I can't believe—" she said as she stared at it and then looked up at him. "We were going to give you ham."

Wade nodded solemnly. "I like ham."

"Yes, but it's nothing like this," Jasmine said as

she looked down at the package in her hands. She felt like she had three thumbs and none of them worked. The ribbon was loosely tied around the package so it should slip off easily. It didn't; she had to yank it off. She should have been able to peel back the tin foil. Instead, she ended up tearing it. But, finally, there in the palm of her hand was an exquisite amber necklace.

"Wherever did you get this?" she whispered. The sun was shining through the kitchen window and it hit the tawny amber and made it sparkle in a dozen different golden hues. "It's beautiful."

Wade ducked his head in acknowledgment. "It belonged to my mother."

"Oh," Jasmine said as she looked up. "That's too precious. I can't—"

Wade just reached out and curled his hand over hers, enclosing the necklace inside her fist. "I want you to have it."

Jasmine felt her eyes get damp. She had managed to not cry when Lonnie threatened to shoot her. She had forced back her tears when she'd been arrested. But this—this was too much.

Then suddenly it hit her and all her tears evaporated. "Is this a goodbye gift?"

The kitchen was warm, but she felt cold.

"No," Wade said, and he took a step closer to her.

She took a step closer, too, and before she knew it she was in his arms and she wasn't even trying to stop her tears.

"I have things I need to figure out." Wade spoke low and close to her ear. It was intimate, like his voice was for her only. "But, I promise you this, if there is any way I can do it, with God's help, I'm going to become a changed man for you."

"I don't—" she interrupted.

He rubbed her neck. "I'll probably always be a little independent. And we'll disagree some. And I know you need to get to know me better. But I've already set up meetings with the pastor. I'm not asking you to wait until I'm done with it all. It's something I need to do on my own. Just me and God. I just want you to know one day soon I'm going to come to you a changed man."

Jasmine nodded. That was all she could manage. She'd wait for him forever, but she couldn't get the words out to tell him that.

"And, when that time comes," he continued in his velvet voice. "I'm going to ask you to marry me."

Jasmine's heart skipped a beat—and then another. She swallowed. Had she heard him right? She didn't need to ask because, by then, he was looking down at her with more tenderness in his face than she'd ever seen on anyone's before.

"Don't answer yet," he murmured.

She couldn't reply if she wanted; she was speechless. But he must have seen by her eyes that her heart was saying yes, because he kissed her. And then, when she thought he was going to pull away, he kissed her again.

Epilogue

The feud between Clarence Sutton and Elmer Maynard did not end during that Christmas dinner. Instead of arguing over fences, however, they started arguing over where Jasmine and Wade were going to get married.

Clarence claimed to be turning his west-facing porch into a large sunroom. He said it was perfect for a wedding dance. On the other hand, Elmer pointed out he had an old tent he planned to use for displaying his cars if he ever went to a car show. He figured it could easily provide seating for every man, woman and child in Dry Creek once he set it up in the grass next to his house.

Neither Jasmine nor Wade bothered joining in the initial conversation or the many that followed. They figured the discussions were good for her father and his grandfather. It connected them in a common goal.

And it gave the bride-to-be and groom-to-be time to make plans of their own. As winter dipped into spring, the two of them grew into the habit of spending the evenings sitting together on the porch Wade's grandfather was getting ready to remodel.

Usually, their conversation revolved around the meetings Wade was having with the pastor and the deep contentment he was finding in his new faith. At other times, they talked about the crops he would be planting when spring came. Wade had agreed to stay with his grandfather and care for the old man and the family farm. Jasmine would join them in the house when they were married.

At first, Jasmine had worried about him giving up his career as a lawman, but he assured her he'd lost his taste for sending people to prison. It was time for him to settle down and do what he'd dreamed of doing as a boy. He wanted to plant and harvest crops.

One of those nights, as they sat on the porch and watched the lights shine out from the cross Jasmine's father had decided to run year-round, the idea struck.

"We could be married up by that cross," Jasmine said. She was snuggled close to Wade in that old quilt so she moved slightly so she could see his face. "It would make a great backdrop for an evening wedding. Just as the sun sets we could say our vows."

Wade smiled. "I like it. Besides, that way half of the wedding guests could sit on Sutton land and the other half on Maynard land."

Jasmine laughed as she settled back into Wade's arms. "Our wedding planners might just agree on the spot, too."

"And that will give us other things to think about. Like this—" Wade said as he bent down and kissed her.

Jasmine wondered how one man could make her heart feel this way. He must have kissed her a few hundred times by now and, each time, it gave her that breathless, knee-bending feeling. Granted some of them were thousand-watt kisses and some of them just glowed steady like this one, but they all moved her just the same. She had no idea love could be like this. It was home and family and desire all wrapped up together. She knew his love would keep her warm for the rest of her life.

* * * * *

Dear Reader,

How important is trust to love? That's the key question that faces Jasmine and Wade in this book. Can we give someone another chance? Can we trust them to do better the next time? Sometimes the answer is yes and sometimes it is no.

Whether we're talking about the love between friends, a man and a woman or family members, we all need to know how important trust is to our love. This decision always seems highlighted to me at Christmas. Each time I write a book, I get reader responses. Last year at Christmas I got several letters from people who said Christmas is always hard for them—and it's because they lost their trust in someone they loved and the holiday feelings brought the situation back to their minds and dampened their enjoyment of the season.

If you find yourself in that situation this Christmas, I want you to know that you are not alone. If possible, find yourself a church family to share. Or volunteer to feed Christmas dinner to the homeless, Or buy a gift for a needy child. There are many ways to share ourselves over the holidays.

I love to hear from my readers. If you get a chance, visit my Web site at www.JanetTronstad.com and send me an e-mail or click in the box on the bottom of the page and go to my Dry Creek Days blog. If you don't have the use of a computer, you may send me a note in care of the editors at Steeple Hill, 233 Broadway, Suite 1001, New York, NY 10279.

Merry Christmas and God Bless You.

Janet Tronstad

QUESTIONS FOR DISCUSSION

1. The people of Dry Creek took a collection to help Wade Sutton because he was out of work. Have you ever needed help like that and been embarrassed to take it? Is there a way the town could have given the money that would have made it easier for Wade to receive it?

2. Wade always had a lot of pride and he tried to keep his poverty a secret as a child. When he looked back as an adult, though, he realized other people were poor, too. Have you ever had a childhood belief challenged as an adult? Can you give an example?

3. To disguise his poverty as a child, Wade made up stories of presents his grandfather gave him and the good food his grandfather made for them on holidays. Have you ever been tempted to pretend things are better than they are?

4. Edith Hargrove-Nelson arranged to pick up Wade every week for Sunday school. Did you have someone in your life who did something similar for you when you were a child?

5. Edith regretted not doing more for Wade. The reporting of child abuse has changed dramatically in the past forty years. If you were in her position today, what would you do? Do you have children in your church who you think might come from abusive homes? What do you do?

6. Jasmine Hunter made her first appearance in *A Dry Creek Courtship.* She came to Dry Creek, looking for her father. She hoped her father wasn't Elmer Maynard, but it was. Did you ever wish someone else was your father or your mother? What qualities did you wish for?

7. Jasmine agreed to be the angel in the Christmas pageant because she wanted to please the people of Dry Creek. What have you done lately to please someone? How do you strike a balance with this in your life?

8. Jasmine also had someone in her past who was not good for her (ex-boyfriend who was in prison). Have you had someone in your life who wasn't good for you? What did you do?

9. Wade had a hard time trusting Jasmine because she was an ex-con. Have you done something in your past that still haunts you? Have you ever had a hard time trusting someone else because of what they've done in the past?

10. Jasmine had difficulty forgiving herself for the past, and even when she became a Christian she still felt she had to do something to deserve it. Has guilt been a problem for you? What would you say to Jasmine at the beginning of the book when she feels this way?

11. Edith Hargrove-Nelson is clearly a strong force in the Dry Creek community. Have you ever been in charge of something like a Christmas pageant? Edith became a little more clipped with people when she was trying to get things done. Do you feel the same when you're doing something like that?

12. Jasmine finally realized Wade just didn't trust her. Can love ever blossom without trust?

When a young Roman woman is wrenched
from the safety of her family and sold into
slavery, she finds herself at the mercy of the
most famous gladiator in Rome. In God's plan,
a master and his slave just might fall in love….

Turn the page for a sneak preview of
THE GLADIATOR
by Carla Capshaw
Available in November 2009
from Love Inspired® Historical

Rome, 81 A.D.

Angry, unfamiliar voices penetrated Pelonia's awareness. Floating between wakefulness and dark, she couldn't budge. Every muscle ached. A sharp pain drummed against her skull.

The voices died away, then a woman's words broke through the haze.

"My name is Lucia. Can you hear me?" The woman pressed a cup of water to Pelonia's cracked lips. "What shall I call you?"

Pelonia coughed as the cool liquid trickled down her arid throat. "Pel...Pelonia."

"Do you remember what happened to you? You were struck on the head and injured. I've been giving you opium to soothe you, but you're far from recovered."

Her eyelids too heavy to open, Pelonia licked her chapped lips.

Gradually her mind began to make sense of her surroundings. The warmth must be sunshine, because the scent of wood smoke hung in the air. Her pallet was a coarse woolen blanket on the hard ground. Dirt clung to her skin and each of her sore muscles longed for the softness of her bed at home.

Home.

Where was she if not in the comfort of her father's Umbrian villa? Who was this woman Lucia? She couldn't remember.

Icy fingers of fear gripped her heart as one by one her memories returned. First the attack, then her father's murder. Raw grief squeezed her chest.

Confusion surrounded her. Where was her uncle? She remembered the slave caravan, his threat to sell her, but nothing more.

Panic forced her eyes open. She managed to focus on the young woman's face above her.

"The master will be here soon." A smile tilted Lucia's thin lips, but didn't touch her honey-brown eyes.

"Where…am I?" she asked, the words grating in her throat.

"You're in the home of Caros Viriathos."

The name meant nothing to Pelonia. She prayed God had delivered her into the hands of a kind man, someone who would help her contact her cousin Tiberia.

Her eyes closed with fatigue. "How…how long have I…been here?"

"Four days and this morning. You've been in and out of sleep. I'll order you a bowl of broth. You should eat to bolster your strength."

Four days, and she remembered nothing. Tiberia must be frantic wondering why she'd failed to attend her wedding.

She opened her eyes. "I must—"

"Don't speak. Now that you've woken, Gaius, our master's steward, says you have one week to recover. Then your labor begins."

"My cousin. I must…"

"You're a slave in the Ludus Maximus now. A possession of the *lanista,* Caros Viriathos."

Lanista? A vile *gladiator* trainer?

"No!"

Lucia crossed her arms over her buxom chest. "We will see."

Heavy footsteps crunched on the rushes strewn across the floor. The new arrival stopped out of Pelonia's view.

The nauseating ache in her head increased

without mercy. What had she done to make God despise her?

Focusing on Lucia, she saw the young woman's face light with pleasure.

"Master," Lucia greeted, jumping to her feet. "The new slave is finally awake. She calls herself Pelonia. She's weak and the medicine I gave her has run its course."

"Then give her more if she needs it."

The man's deep voice poured over Pelonia like the soothing water of a bath. She turned her head, ignoring the jab of pain that pierced her skull.

"You mustn't move your head," Lucia snapped, "or you might injure yourself further."

Pelonia stiffened. She wasn't accustomed to taking orders from slaves.

Lucia glanced toward the door. "She's argumentative. I have a hunch she'll be difficult. She denies she's your slave."

Silence followed Lucia's remark. Would this man who claimed to own her kill or beat her? Was he a cruel barbarian?

She sensed him move closer. Her tension rose as if she were prey in the sights of a hungry lion. At last the lion crossed to where she could see him.

Sunlight streaming through the window enveloped the giant, giving his dark hair a golden glow. A crisp, light-colored tunic draped across his shoulders and chest contrasted sharply with the rich copper of his skin. Gold bands around his upper arms emphasized the thickness of his muscles, the physical power he held in check.

Her breath hitched in her throat. She could only stare. Without a doubt, the man could crush her if he chose.

"So, you are called Pelonia," he said. "And my healer believes you wish to fight me."

Her gaze locked with the unusual blue of his forceful glare. For the first time she understood how the Hebrew, David, must have suffered when he faced Goliath. Swallowing the lump of fear in her throat, she nodded. "If I must."

"If you must?" Caros eyed Pelonia with a mix of irritation and respect. With her tunic filthy and torn, her dark hair in disarray and her bruises healing, his new slave looked like a wounded goddess. But she was just an ordinary woman. Why did she think she could defy him?

"Then let the games begin," he said, his voice thick with mockery.

"You think…this…this is a game?" she asked faintly.

The roughness of her voice reminded him of her body's weakened condition—a frailty her spirit clearly didn't share. Crouching beside her, he ran his forefinger over the yellowed bruise on her cheek. She closed her eyes and sighed as though his touch somehow soothed her.

Her guileless response unnerved him. The need to protect her enveloped him, a sensation he hadn't known since the deaths of his mother and sisters. As a slave, he'd been beaten on many occasions in an effort to conquer his will. That no one ever succeeded was a matter of pride for him. Much to his surprise, he had no wish to see this girl broken, either.

"Of course it's a game. And I will be the victor."

Defiance flamed in the depths of her large, doe-brown eyes. She didn't speak and he admired her restraint when he could see she wanted to flay him.

"You might as well give in now, my prize. I own you whether you will it or not."

He gripped her chin and forced her to look at him.

"Admit it," he said. "Then you can return to your sleep."

She shook her head. "No. No one owns me...no one but my God."

"And who might your god be? Jupiter? Apollo? Or maybe you worship the god of the sea. Do you think Neptune will rescue you?"

"The Christ."

Caros wondered if she were a fool or had a wish for death. "Say that to the wrong person, Pelonia, and you'll find yourself facing the lions."

"I already am."

He laughed. "So you think of me as a ferocious beast?"

Her silence amused him all the more. "Good. It suits me well to know you realize I'm untamed and capable of tearing you limb from limb."

"Then do your worst. Death is better…than being owned."

Caros suddenly noticed Pelonia had grown pale and weaker still.

He berated himself for depleting her meager strength when he should have been encouraging her to heal. He lifted her into his arms.

She weighed no more than a laurel leaf. Had he pushed her to the brink of death?

Holding her tight against his chest, he whispered near her ear. "Tell me, *mea carissima*. What can I do to aid you? What can I do to ease your plight?"

"Find…Tiberia," she whispered, the dregs of her strength draining away. "And free me."

* * * * *

Will Pelonia ever convince Caros of who she
is and where she truly belongs? Or will their
growing love bind her to him for all time?

Find out in
THE GLADIATOR
by Carla Capshaw.
Available in November 2009
from Love Inspired® Historical.

Love Inspired® SUSPENSE

RIVETING INSPIRATIONAL ROMANCE

Watch for our new series of
edge-of-your-seat suspense novels.
These contemporary tales
of intrigue and romance
feature Christian characters
facing challenges to their faith...
and their lives!

Steeple
Hill®

Visit:

Love Inspired.
HISTORICAL
INSPIRATIONAL HISTORICAL ROMANCE

Engaging stories of romance,
adventure and faith,
these novels are set in
various historical periods
from biblical times
to World War II.

NOW AVAILABLE!

Steeple
Hill®